EMANCIPATION

by

Michael R. Lane

To my mother, Elizabeth, for all the things I may do to make you proud, they will never amount to how proud I am of you. In memory of the pioneer of Strawberry Hill Press, Dr. Jean-Louis Brindamour: friend, teacher, writer, scholar, and counselor, may you rest in peace.

Love, Michael

STORY ONE

Standing dormant, in the peaceful shadow of time
-- The Prophet

On a bright dog day beneath Kaufmann's Roman-numeral clock stands a long-whiskered, head-bowed man in a seedy black wool coat and unfastened galoshes. At noon, his head levels and he bounds out of the clock's shadow to the curb. Pounding his cougar-head walking stick three times on the sidewalk, he waits, as a maestro awaits silence from his audience.

"Sinners!" he erupts, "The Day of Judgment draws near!"

"Get lost, asshole!" "Shut up!" come the cries as people maneuver around. "Go back to the nut farm, you jerk!"

His head lifts higher. His fierce brown eyes defiantly watch a hectic four-way intersection. Everywhere are people in light-colored polyesters, sleeveless blouses, terrycloth shorts, T-shirts, leather sandals, and opaque sunglasses. Abruptly he speaks, this time louder: "The Lord has said for thee to right thy wicked ways or face his merciless wrath!"

"Go home, bum!" a teenage boy shouts as he enters Kaufmann's through revolving glass doors.

"And still you heed not his warnings!" the man continued unperturbed. "Going about in your vile, accursed ways, like shameless pigs in slop, trusting in the feeble, grounded works of man over thy heavenly Father, who loves thee more than his only Son! For this blasphemous atrocity, he has damned your unpardonable souls for all eternity!"

"Hey! Watch it fool!" a short man shouts nearly struck by the orator's pointing finger.

"Watch the heavens!" replies The Prophet. "For the Lord shall rain his vengeance on you if you do not repent!"

Curious eyes watch as he stamps his feet, flails his arms, and alternately points his walking stick at them and the hazy sky. His sermon bellows with the fever pitch of a Baptist minister, climaxing by singing, with tearful eyes, a dirge to the sun.

At precisely one o'clock, he stops as if ordered by his Lord to do so, and pensively returns to the shadows. Nudging a middle-aged woman out of the way, he settles in, a holy man moribundly staring straight ahead. His callused hands comfortably fold atop the cougar-head stick. Slowly, his head bows and his eyes shut. Those who had not witnessed his revival would never suspect him, standing dormant, in the peaceful shadow of time, to be capable of such a tirade.

****

"How's he doin' Doc?"

"Not good Sarge, bullet's gone clean through, trying to stop the bleeding now."

Gratey chewed noisily on three pieces of Bazooka bubble gum that had lost their flavor half an hour ago, as Sgt. Chip Saunders gave Littlejohn a sympathetic glance, then looked back at Doc. "We can't stay here; Krauts'll be back any minute."

K Company's best, along with a hotshot by the name of Kolvac, had successfully infiltrated enemy territory, and Gratey watched them for each dangerous moment it took to get there. K Company was trapped in an abandoned two-story building that the Germans were using as temporary headquarters. Sgt. Saunders looked toward the open front door. Gratey leaned closer as the camera caught a close-up of the Sergeant's stubbled profile.

Belly down on the cool linoleum floor, face propped in the bevel of his two delicate hands, two feet from the nineteen-inch black-and-white Philco, Gratey watched intently. He dreamed of one day being like Sgt. Saunders, tough and fearless. No matter what the situation, The Sarge, as Gratey called him, faced and conquered it, oftentimes with enough left over for one of his smiles that resembled a sneer. It was the superhuman ability of The Sarge to break the wild steed of danger that made Gratey certain of one thing. In nine years, only because it was not possible sooner, he would join the United States Army.

At the far end of a collapsing porch, Nelson lit a cigarette. Gratey chewed slowly. He could sense something was about to happen. Nelson looked down the only road in and out of the ghost town. The camera panned the street, nothing but dust and a few long deserted buildings. Taking a couple of steps to his right Nelson stilled and listened. Gratey heard the faint distinct sound of military vehicles. *The Germans*, Gratey thought. Nelson ran inside.

"Someone's coming," Nelson said.

The Sarge ordered the men into the basement.

"What about Littlejohn?" Doc asked.

"I'll take care of him," The Sarge said. "Get goin'."

Sgt. Saunders lifted Littlejohn and draped the giant over his shoulder. "That's what I would've done," Gratey whispered. For the first time, Littlejohn moaned in pain.

A jeep squealed to a halt followed closely by an armored truck. From the jeep stepped an arrogant German lieutenant. Gratey knew he was a lieutenant. He recognized the markings on his uniform from books he had read on military insignias.

The lieutenant barked out orders in German. Four German infantrymen converged on the house. Gratey blew a bubble and burst it with his tongue. Camille laughed. Gratey looked over his shoulder at his baby sister. She was smiling, showcasing all of her two front teeth. Camille reached over the top rail of her crib with one hand and balanced herself against the rail with the other. Gratey stuck out his tongue. Camille looked amazed. Gratey grinned and returned to watching "Combat."

The scene had switched to a makeshift American headquarters.

"You know that letter Kolvac got?" Lt. Hanley asked Caje.

"Yeah," Caje said while smoking a cigarette looking very tense.

"It's on the level," Lt. Hanley said. "His wife's dying." Music blared as the scene went to black.

Gratey stood and turned down the volume. He picked up his model rocket launch pad that was near his feet intending to return it to his room. Earlier that day he had lost his Scorpion rocket. It was caught in a strong wind upon its descent and carried onto a rooftop near the empty grass lot he used as his Cape Canaveral. Since it was his least favorite and least expensive model rocket, he swiftly dismissed the experience.

"Okay little girl let's check you out," Gratey said as he walked up to the crib. Gratey put the launch pad on the floor next to an empty Ivory Snow box at the foot of the crib. From its wooden platform, the launch pad's metal guide rod was as high as Gratey's hip. Camille falsely anticipated Gratey was about to lift her and stretched out her arms. "No you don't." Gratey peeled her chubby arms from about his neck and placed Camille on her back. "Now let's see if she pooh-pooh or pee-pee."

Gratey unpinned the diaper and found it unsoiled. Making certain the points of the safety pins faced away from his baby sister's body, Gratey snugly pinned back the diaper.

"Hey little lady," Gratey said as he rubbed Camille's belly, "you're dry as dust." Camille tried to stuff one of her fists into her mouth. Gratey kissed her on each cheek and handed her Pepper, a cocoa-faced, black-yarn-haired, Raggedy Ann doll her mother had made for her. It took Camille one week to rip off one of the brown button eyes. Camille hugged Pepper then stared at her face. For a moment, Gratey watched Camille amuse herself with the doll, then stole away to his parents' bedroom door four steps behind the crib, tossing his leathery gum into the Ivory Snow box.

The door was slightly ajar. Gratey eased it open but remained outside. His father had a dark, massive arm laid to rest across the bare, thin shoulder of his mother, his large face nuzzled in the tiny nape of her neck, a contrast of coal and bronze in the late evening light.

From the open window floated an uneven blend of sounds from Centre Avenue. Three hours ago, his father had just gotten home from double shifts at the rail yards, the third in four days. Josephine Johnson could not sleep without her husband. She spent those lonely nights sewing, cleaning, reading, and listening to the radio. After Carl Johnson ate, he made love to his wife. Shortly thereafter, Gratey returned from his daylong visit with his best friend Tracy Cox and found his parents asleep.

Tracy had told Gratey, in very excited terms that he was going to Fresh Air Camp in two weeks. According to Tracy, there were still a few spots left. Gratey dreamed of going to a summer camp, and with Tracy along it was guaranteed fun.

The deadline was Friday. That gave Gratey two days. He couldn't wait. He needed to know now if his parents could afford the fifty dollars it cost to send him, if they decided he could go at all.

Gratey looked back at the crib as if he might find the answers there. Camille had stood and was looking down into the Ivory Snow box until she noticed Gratey staring at her. Camille reached for Gratey with both hands. Her bottom lip poked out. Camille was about to cry. Gratey pressed a finger to his lips, signaling Camille to silence. She seemed to understand but kept reaching.

Gratey tiptoed inside to his father's side of the bed. After Gratey licked his lips, he leaned over and whispered, "Dad." All Gratey heard in response was a low snore. "Dad," Gratey whispered again. Not even an eyelash moved. Gratey reached down and was about to shake his father when he heard a loud thud come from the living room. Gratey straightened his back, his hands still poised to shake his father. *Camille's thrown Pepper on the floor again*, he thought, only able to see a small corner of the crib through the wide-open bedroom door. Gratey looked back and forth between what he could see of the crib and his father. *Maybe it would be better to wait*, Gratey thought, dropping his hands to his sides and his courage onto the pillow near the reposed face of his dad. On tiptoe, Gratey left his parents' bedroom and eased shut the door behind him.

"Camille," Gratey said as he stepped toward the crib. The first thing he noticed was Camille was not in her crib. Gratey looked around. He saw Camille impaled on his rocket launcher, blood trickling from her nose and ears. The metal rod had punched clear through her temple. Her body had constricted like a snail into its shell as it did sometimes when she slept. Gratey knelt beside Camille on one knee. Her eyes were wide open as if she saw something that terrified her. The right side of her face was a sickening black and blue. Gratey made one, two, three attempts before he could touch Camille, and when he did, his hand recoiled as if his baby sister were on fire. Camille wasn't breathing. His disbelieving eyes moved from Camille to Pepper, perched lopsidedly against the worn round bars of the crib, staring blindly back at him with one button eye. For a moment, a fidgety smile replaced his gaped mouth until his eyes fell back upon Camille.

With a hurried stagger, Gratey made his way into his parents' bedroom. "What's wrong Gratey?" his mother drowsily asked as Gratey violently shook the plank-wide shoulders of his father: "Camille . . . she fell . . . hurt . . . bad." Gratey couldn't find the words or complete the thought. His father swept by him in a panicked rush for the living room. Mrs. Johnson held Gratey's sorrowful stare. "Dear God no!" came the cry from the living room. His mother leaped from the bed wearing nothing, just as his father began a frantic litany of pleas for Camille to awaken.

****

Gratey had not moved. He had lapsed into a coma-like trance, a self-taught state of reflection and meditation. Upon the screen behind his closed eyelids, Gratey relived the incident that had scarred his childhood. His father, wearing only his white boxer shorts, cradling Camille, pleading with her to breathe, cry, make any life sound. His mother as naked and vulnerable as a newborn infant wailed and blubbered and prayed for mercy and for God to give their baby one more chance.

Gratey had found himself leaning back against the bedroom door, sobbing, afraid to move but wanting to escape. Each guttural wail from his mother had made his chest tighten, his sobbing more intense. "I'm sorry," Gratey had said, at first in his mind then as a hoarse whisper from trembling lips that no one but Gratey heard.

Fresh tears snaked along Gratey Johnson's narrow cheeks into the thick webbing of his beard. His hands squeezed the cougar-head of his walking stick with a force that threatened to crush it. The cacophony of his mother's wails and his father's pleas built to a maddening crescendo. He mouthed the words, "I'm sorry," over and over and over again. Then, as if some huge hand covered his interior eyes, the memory vanished behind an impenetrable fog and returned to its permanent storage place in his soul.

STORY TWO

His right foot pressed flat against the corner stone
-- Curtiss Christopher Warrin

Serious fool, Curtiss thought as he stared at The Prophet from across the street. His right foot pressed flat against the corner stone of the Mellon Building; one hand rested on his bent knee, the other hung nonchalantly by his side. He managed to survey all around him by moving only his shielded eyes, his head erect and as fixed as the stone.

As always, Curtiss wore mirrored sunglasses. "Day or night, winter through spring, you won't catch Cool Curt without his silver shades," homeboys would say, "'cause Curt is def', hapnin', chilly. He don't sweat and he don't fret."

Most homegirls felt differently. They believed it was because of his lucid gray eyes. Those unique features -- in salutary unison with his daddy's taut peach skin stretched across angular jaws, generous forehead, powerful chin; stoked by an innate confidence, brashly displayed in the effortless movements of his athletic, six-foot frame -- had made him desirable to practically every girl at predominantly black Salvation High School.

Whether at his recent alma mater, the Pilazzo Pizza Parlor where he worked part-time as a pizza maker, watching television, or at the movies, Curtiss was certain to be wearing a pair of mirrored shades. He collected them, had one dresser drawer filled exclusively with them. As a number of girls could testify, Curtiss even made love with them on. It was rumored by students at Salvation High that the only time he ever took them off was to fight or sleep. Both Curtiss and his close friends knew that to be an exaggeration, but they saw no harm in allowing the myth to perpetuate itself. Besides, Curtiss enjoyed the reputation.

The truth is Curtiss got his first pair of sunglasses from his father when he was six. Those cheap kind parents often embarrass their children with, a pair with white plastic frames and shiny silver lenses. Curtiss wore them all day and night, including to bed. Next day, he was told the news of his father's murder. "Killed by a mugger," the muscular cop told his mother. "He probably resisted," the skinny cop added, gnawing relentlessly on a stogie, looking around their little plaster house, squinting with disapproval.

People in the black community knew different. They believed Frank Warrin was murdered by the police and for good reasons: his unflinching opposition to an administration whose unmasked racist policies he brazenly defied with ardent speeches and unauthorized demonstrations that often escalated into violent confrontations with the police. Support groups formed in both the minority and liberal communities. Numbers increased along with outspoken, active participants. The mayor tried diluting the situation with threats of imprisonment and unrestrained police force, calling Curtiss's father "a subversive, radical tyrant." Frank Warrin laughed when he read it in The Pittsburgh Press, telling a crowd of supporters at the New Day rally that he honestly did not believe the mayor knew what those words meant.

When seeking the killers of Frank Warrin, the police focused their investigation solely in the poor black community of the Hill District, since it was in an alley behind Fifth Avenue High School where the body was found. Two young black men, Wilbur Heritage and Matson Creek, who were known members of The Black Panther Party, were convicted of his murder in spite of demands for an internal police investigation and the impeachment of the mayor.

Some of the more vocally persistent in those matters were arrested by a blizzard of police abuse and harassment that served to snuff out the hot coals of rebellion with only a few vehement hisses.

The suppression did not last. It was the time of Dr. King and Malcolm X, a period when Watts would go up in flames, a president of the United States and a future hopeful would be assassinated, when Vietnam, acid, rock 'n' roll, love-ins, and sit-ins were the fare of the day. A time when passive activists and vocal multitudes demanded

13

America lived up to her creed for all her citizens. In those times, when the ambiguous question of right would not be vanquished, a nation met its past, in the face of its future, and was served notice the time of change was long overdue.

In retrospect, the death of his father was destiny. A conclusion he drew for himself at age fifteen. Still the pain and hate for those who believed they had the right to extinguish his life would not leave him. Only smolder and perhaps erupt one unforeseen day.

They buried Franklin Moses Warrin at Allegheny Cemetery, where most Korean War veterans who lived in Allegheny County were buried. Curtiss wore his plastic sunglasses. His mother attempted to take them away but he fought, kicked, screamed, and hollered so much that she gave up. With an angered, dry face, he watched them lower the casket into the ground. Silently, he said goodbye, firmly held the quivering hand of his mother, and began his ascent into manhood.

Curtiss worked a wooden toothpick from one side of his mouth to the other. Cars and buses moved laboriously up and down Fifth Avenue, ejecting noxious fumes into the oppressive afternoon air. As Curtiss watched The Prophet, he made unconscious comparisons between the shabby preacher and his murdered father. They looked nothing alike: his dad, a sinewy, light-complexioned man with wavy black hair, clean-shaven, preferred suits and ties. Like The Prophet, his father had delivered his speeches as if he were an attorney in closing argument, making one final radical plea to save his client from a penalty of death.

Unlike The Prophet, his father wanted black people to stand up for themselves and fight back with knowledge and inner strength. "Become accountable for your own futures," he had often said. "Black pride and dignity is what the community needs; not more cops or drug dealers, numbers-runners, bars and pool halls, or Mercedes-driving preachers." He had wanted them to get up off their knees and stop praying to some invisible, merciless, self-righteous God and place that faith -- they so eagerly surrendered -- in themselves and each other. "There's your God people," he would say, "Unity!"

Two-thirteen, Kaufmann's roman-numeral clock read. Most of the throng had returned to work, leaving steady streams of sluggish shoppers to leisurely patrol the bright downtown streets. With mild curiosity, Curtiss watched a teenage boy in an apparently confused state, wait at an intersection cater-corner to where he stood. Half of the boy's wrinkled, striped, short-sleeved shirt was tucked in his crumpled pants; the other half, frayed at the edge, lay helplessly on his flabby hip. From his uncoordinated manner and ingrained expression of confused imbecility, he appeared to Curtiss to be mentally retarded. On the boy's flushed, swollen wrist, Curtiss saw the glint of a gold watch. What if someone tried to rip him off? What would he do? Then as if shaken by a tremor of genius, Curtiss concluded: The same thing I would probably -- give up the watch.

A stocky man with dark hair and tanned skin, carrying a stained leather rifle case (weighted with what Curtiss assumed was a rifle) stopped before him. There was a pinch of something Curtiss noticed about him, like a flash or vision out of the corner of one's eye. Curtiss tilted his head slightly forward and peered over the top of his sunglasses. In the unfiltered sunlight, he could see the man had gray eyes, although a darker and denser gray than his own. The man noticed Curtiss looking at him, smiled generously, nodded his head in greeting, looked with uncertainty left, then right, and made a brisk decision to go to his right, eventually waiting at the corner. Curtiss watched, oddly amused by the discovery of kindred eyes as he leaned his head back against the wall.

In some fictional story he had to read for old Mrs. Martin as an English assignment, the narrator mentioned that gray eyes were keenest and that all famous sharpshooters had them. True, he did have exceptional vision (fifteen in his right eye, twenty in his left). This raised the very serious possibility of him becoming a sharpshooter, the single occupation earmarked by an Army recruiter he went to see on his sixteenth birthday two years ago.

To Curtiss, sighting something through a riflescope was nothing new. He had used his M-16 BB rifle on neighborhood pigeons and rats. After he squeezed the trigger, he would watch squeamishly. Most of the times, what he saw was a wounded creature that usually made a pained escape. Curtiss did not know if he was capable of doing that to another human being. He told the recruiter he would think about it. That was before he visited his Uncle Jimmy in Alabama.

For the first time in his life, Curtiss boarded a plane. He did not lug with him any of the typical novice fears or excited expectations. Only a dire request from his mother for him to visit with the sole surviving brother of his late father, a man who claimed Curtiss as his favorite nephew but had only seen him once when he was three.

The plane hummed above the clouds. Curtiss looked out of his window and squinted from the glare of an undaunted sun. When he looked down Curtiss saw, glistening in every direction, an infinite ocean of white ambling toward the curve of infinity. From up there, unbounded and serene, a peculiar mood of universal unity and humility subdued him. A calm he had never known nested in his soul. This must be God's view Curtiss reasoned. This must be the place for me. It was then, during what his mother would have called a religious experience that Curtiss decided to join the Air Force.

In all, his visit was pleasant. He got to know his cousins. Though slow to his way of thinking, they were agreeable and fun. His uncle, who was obviously ill (although he never made clear what ailment he had), seemed to grapple with pain itself as he told Curtiss a bushel of stories of when he was a boy, some of which he absentmindedly repeated.

One that Curtiss found particularly interesting, no matter how many times he heard it, was the disappearance of Uncle Jimmy's Aunt Josephine.

"When I was 'bout six," Uncle Jimmy always began one of his stories with his approximate age, "I happened on mama sittin' on the back stoop starin' out into nothin'. It was one of them hot Alabama afternoons and I wouldn't ah thought nothin' 'bout it, 'cept she was wearin' Grandma May's ol' knitted shawl. Had it wrapped tight 'round her shoulders like she was freezin'.

"Now I watched mama for a minute, tryin' to decipher if I was prepared to step up and ask her why she was wearin' Grandma May's shawl on such a hot day, but somethin' held me back. Swear to Jesus it was like someone grabbed me by the back of my trousers and would not so much as let me fall forward, let 'lone walk. I took that as a sign mama wasn't supposed to be disturbed. Course I didn't know that then, bein' only six and all. But that's what it was all right boy, a sign from God."

Curtiss disliked being called "boy," but since Uncle Jimmy and Aunt Effie often referred to their own sons in the same affectionate manner, it made it less of an insult and more of a term of acceptance into their part of the family.

"I keep an eye on mama for a while 'fore I starts gettin' worried. Mama wasn't movin'. Jus' kept starin' at nothin'.

"I makes my way to the front of the house and sees daddy. He jus' finished eatin' lunch and was goin' rest a bit on the front porch swing before he went back out in the fields. I knows I ain't supposed to disturb daddy but this was important.

"Daddy, I says it real quiet almost like a whisper, what's wrong with mama?

"What you mean boy? Ain't nothin' wrong with your mama, my daddy says. He don't sound upset so I knows it okay to go on: she actin' funny.

"Get to the point Little Jim. He called me Little Jim 'cause I was a runt when I was born. Anyways, I tell daddy what I saw. You never seen Grandpa Warrin did you, boy?"

Curtiss always answered with a slow swivel of his head. It seemed to maintain the suspenseful mood Uncle Jimmy had so carefully developed.

"He was somethin'. Gentle Giant folks used to call him. Had the meanest looks you ever laid eyes on. Mama told him one time he looked like he swallowed a fistful of uncooked salt pork. That's the way he looked when I asked him that question 'bout mama. 'Cept instead of mean, his eyes kind of fell back like when you thinkin' 'bout somethin' real sorrowful. His face drops a little. Next thing I know daddy lookin' down in his lap at his hands tellin' me this story 'bout mama and her baby sister I ain't never heard nothin' 'bout."

This was the part Curtiss enjoyed the most, when Uncle Jimmy leaned in close and spoke in hushed tones: "Seems mama had a baby sister name of Josephine that run off when she was fifteen on account of some argument they had 'bout who's turn it was to do laundry. Mama didn't think much 'bout it then, daddy said, 'cause they was always havin' arguments 'bout one thing or another, and Josephine been threatenin' to run off ever since she was ten. But mama's baby sister run off that day and never came back.

"Daddy said a cousin Daniel, who moved to Philadelphia a few years before this happened, wrote mama a letter that said he'd seen Josey (that's what family called her). She had checked into the boardin' house he was workin' at with a man claimed to be her husband. Johnson was his name, don't remember his first. Daniel said in the letter that they had a little boy with 'em. What was his name? Gary or George, somethin' begin with a G.

"Daddy said they went north to see if they could find her. By the time they got there, cousin Daniel said they'd long gone. Daniel didn't have a clue where they might be headed. He was real sorry too, but Daniel didn't know Josey had run away. Daniel told daddy, Josey and her family was on there way to visit her husband's kin, he had no reason to suspect otherwise.

"That's as close as mama ever came to catchin' up to Josey. 'Til this very day, every year, on the day Josey ran away, mama'll wrap herself up in Grandma May's shawl, sit on the back stoop and jus' stare out into nothin'. Guess she still believe Josey's coming back home one day.

"You don't know nobody name of Josey or Josephine do you boy?"

Curtiss would answer no.

"Well, if you do meet somebody with that name, 'bout sixty or so, she might jus' be your great-aunt."

Curtiss would smile at the thought of such a discovery, keeping in mind what Aunt Effie had said: "Your Uncle Jimmy can turn a tale both true and false. There's times -- not meanin' to mind you -- he kind of mixes up the two."

It didn't matter. As much as Curtiss enjoyed the stories Uncle Jimmy told, Curtiss enjoyed the familiar passion in his uncle's brown eyes even more. His hair and nose were those of Curtiss's father. His voice was deeper, his skin darker, but there were certain unnerving similarities. The way he reached for things with a studied, cautious hand. How he would stare as if there were always something to be seen through whatever it was he was looking at. How his nose wrinkled as he spoke of unpleasant experiences or the forceful way he poked out his bottom lip.

Then there was his laugh. A volcanic laugh that mixed, blended, and then exploded as a volatile concoction of unencumbered freedom, making even the most stolid victim to its joviality. A laugh that did not die in its absence, but echoed heartily in the memories of every person whose ear it touched. This, too, was his father's laugh, and in private, a laugh that made him weep.

And so he left his uncle, Aunt Effie, and his cousins with unanticipated sorrow. A sorrow he would not feel upon leaving Pittsburgh. If only Manijeh would agree to go with him.

STORY THREE

My first love, my only lover
-- Manijeh "Mannie" Lovejoy

Another pack of wolves, days like this bring them out of the woodwork. I'll cut down Grant, shoot into Gimbel's, pick up Curtiss's going away present, and go home. All this running around -- to the grocery store for mom, getting dad's birthday present, picking up my school books -- and this thing with Curtiss have got me worn out.

What am I going to tell Curtiss? Thanks for the offer but no thanks. Yes, I love you, but I made plans to go to Pitt and become a doctor years before we met, and now you're trying to stop up the works with your love. Have a nice boot camp. Don't forget to write. Shut up Mannie, you're getting dumber by the minute.

At least Gimbel's isn't crowded. Air conditioning feels nice. Maybe I'll tell him after Ty's party tonight. I don't know, breaks my heart to think about it.

Uh-oh, crazy Clip wondering around. No telling what he's up to. Hope he didn't see me. "Hold the elevator!" Don't look back he might've recognized your voice. "Thank you."

Last thing I need is Clip following me around like some abandoned rebel, babbling on about one of his spaced-out theories on evolution or psychology or philosophy or Colonel Sanders or whatever. I can't handle that stuff right now. The boy is weird, kind of a cross between an egghead and a thug. I can't figure him out. Doubt if he can figure himself out half the time.

Curtiss's bracelet should be ready by now. The engraver said he'd have it done in an hour. White gold, expensive but Curtiss is worth it. It'll give him something special to remember us by. Dad's going to kill me when he sees it on his charge.

"Hi. I'm here to pick up the bracelet I left for engraving."

"Name?"

"Manijeh Lovejoy." Hope this guy was able to get the whole thing on there. "That's it."

"I couldn't get all of The Summer of '88 like you wanted. I dropped the The. Hope you don't mind?"

I hope he didn't screw it up. It feels so light, almost weightless; Summer of '88, the best summer of my life.

"If you don't like it, we can replace it for you within an hour."

"It's perfect. How much do I owe you?"

"Engraving's free with the purchase, ma'am."

My father has a favorite joke. He tells it every Sunday (when he thinks my mother and my sister and me can't hear him) to his beer-drinking buddies, while they watch afternoon sports on television. "When I die," his voice is serious like when he argues one of those court cases for Westinghouse Electric, "let it be while making love to my sweet Sandy" (my mother, his wife).

Someone, usually sleepy-eyed Mr. Colefield, acting like my dad's melon-head straight man as mom sometimes calls him, will ask, "Why's that Russel?" My father kind of leans his Rosey Grier body forward, looks at Mr. Colefield's inquisitive mask and delivers that worn-out punch line: "That way, I'll be cumming and going at the same time."

They laugh as if it was the first time they'd ever heard the stupid thing. It's never been funny to me and I've overheard him tell it at least a hundred times. That's a disgusting thing to say about someone you love. If I ever hear my man say something like that about me, he'll find himself sleeping with one of those beer-bellied fools.

That has nothing to do with Curtiss and me at least I don't think so.

Curtiss wants to get married, that part I can handle. But it means I'd have to go with him, change all of my plans, leave Pittsburgh, my family, and all of my friends. I tell Curtiss I'm already enrolled at Pitt and try to explain to him why it's so important to me. He tells me there are colleges in San Antonio like my words just fell on the floor between my mouth and his ears. He asks me, "What's so special about Pitt?" After I think on it for a minute, I try explaining to Curtiss that it's not only Pitt but Pittsburgh I find special. I've been a few places: New York, Philly, L.A., Atlanta, Chi-town, and some of the other so-called happenin' spots. None of them had the city-town flavor of The 'Burgh that makes me feel . . . comfortable. They were, for lack of a better term, nice places to visit.

Curtiss says that's bullshit. I don't argue. I didn't tell him it was bullshit when he told me the story about why he always wears sunglasses. I didn't belittle him when he made this huge production out of taking them off, "Just for you babe." I do what I've trained myself to do for the last couple of months, quietly take it on the chin, mentally cover up, and try to figure out why it is so difficult for him to understand my feelings about The 'Burgh.

Yesterday frightened me. Curtiss gave me an ultimatum: "I'm leaving for boot camp in thirteen days and I'm not coming back." Then he looks at me, barefaced, those gray eyes melting away my stubbornness. "I don't know Curtiss," I keep saying. But sadly, I do.

From the first time I saw Curtiss walk down the hall in ninth grade, I've been digging on him. He was skinny then -- actually more like lean. But he had what my mother would call a commanding presence. It was as if he owned the halls. Not the way jocks or bullies do it by loping or exaggerating every movement. Curtiss had more grace than that. It was as if he were saying with each step, "I'm somebody special. I know it and so do you."

Nobody messed with him either. I couldn't figure that out until I saw Curtiss and Walter go at it. Walter Worlds had at least fifty pounds and five inches on Curtiss. Curtiss ate him up. He left Walter on the ground, bleeding and moaning in the dirt. Curtiss retrieved his shades from Robinelle (that was his lady then), put his arm around her and walked away as if it was everyday moves.

For me it wasn't the fighting, or the fact that Curtiss wasn't afraid to fight somebody like Walter that I was digging. I think fighting is for fools and morons. But the way Curtiss went about it. No yelling, screaming, loud name calling, only, let's do it. And man did he ever.

That was also the first close look I got at those legendary eyes. Light gray with long, black lashes. Those were, without a doubt, the most heavenly eyes I had ever seen.

"Hey baby, check this out."

"Buzz off clown!"

"Wait a minute, sweetheart! Why you wanna be so mean?"

"I'm not your sweetheart."

"Come on back here and I'll give you something that'll make you sweet!"

"Right, right, whatever."

Every time I come downtown, I have to deal with the same nonsense. "Hey baby, check this out. Hey sugar, let me talk to you for a minute. Hey girlie girl! YO! Miss Diamond! I'd love to polish your karats." Who cares! Can't these fools leave me alone for once?

Who am I kidding? By eleventh grade, I'd gone through a basketball player, a football player, a track star; one self-pitying bully (not Walter), one Fine Brother, and a pseudo intellectual from Shadyside Academy. They all shared three things: over inflated egos (bully not excluded), being pests to the highest degree, and a serious penchant for ignoring the meaning of the word no. Sterling captains of the jerkian core.

Up until my junior year, Curtiss said no more to me than "hi" and "how are you?" He never asked me out, walked me down the hall, joked with, laughed at, or picked on me as I'd hoped he would. I talked to mom about him, and she said, "If he won't come to you, that leaves just one alternative. You're going to have to make the first move."

Me make the first move! I thought mom was tripping. No way was I going to make the first move on any man. Until she told me that was how she met my father, then suddenly the idea didn't seem as bad.

So, on a clear, windy day, one week before Thanksgiving, I told Girlfriend (that's my best girl Sheila) "Today, I'm going to ask Curtiss Warrin out."

"Go 'head girl!" Sheila says, all excited, like it was her going to ask Curtiss out. I just look at her, giving her my don't-even-think-about-it stare, and talk on.

"I heard he split with Debbie --"

"Who ain't?" Sheila says before I can finish. "What he ever see in her?" She asks me like I got the National Enquirer. I tell her I don't know, but really, I do.

Debbie is cute, no doubt about that, but the chick is so stuck on herself. Me and girlfriend started calling her Velcro. Debbie always had her face in the bathroom mirror touching up this, lining that. Sticking out those tiny titties and that narrow ass, trying to make them look bigger than they were.

"Glad he cut that cord," Sheila goes on. Me, I'm still waiting for my chance to finish what I have to say. But that's Girlfriend, she'll talk you to death if you let her.

"When you gonna ask him?" Sheila finally gets around to saying.

"After the football game," I tell her, and then I let her in on the plan. Sheila's grinning and hugging me like I just won the lottery, then she starts in with one of her pep talks.

Me and Sheila were both cheerleaders. I did it because . . . I don't know why I did it. But Sheila, she's a natural, forever the cheery optimist. Whatever's wrong just give 'em an s-m-i-l-e and it'll be all right. I mean the girl religiously watches Disney, and I wouldn't be surprised if she still believes in Santa Claus. But she's good people and I love her.

That day at the game, I showed off my best moves: jumped a little higher, smiled a little brighter, and added a few more splits.

Curtiss was sitting in what cheerleaders call F.B. Row. The F.B. stands for Fine Brothers. A Fine Brother is not just good-looking. He is supposed to have style, class, and a smooth, controlled manner. "Sharp and sweet," as my baby sister would say. Kent had been the only F.B. I ever dated. We lasted about two months. That was two months too long.

Salvation was once again getting their behinds whipped, 48 to 17. There were 43 seconds left in the game. Peabody had the ball on our 29-yard line and we were giving the home fans our Mercy cheer:

Block that kick!
Intercept that ball!
Mercy! Please!
Don't let them score!

24

Sheila hated that cheer. Her man was the team quarterback. Duncan is cute, but slow as cardboard. I doubt if the boy can count past one hundred or memorize his address. I don't tell Sheila this because I hate hurting her feelings, besides, they are down with each other. He didn't mess around like the majority of his teammates did, and he treats her like she's the best thing since rap music, so who am I to say.

As soon as the gun sounded, I picked up my pompoms and bounced over to Exit C, where the Fine Brothers would be coming out.

I've always been attractive, not cute, or pretty, but show-stopping lovely. Not bragging, just fact. But I don't put much weight in it because I prefer using my brain. Until this day, I can't believe the way I fell apart trying to ask Curtiss out.

Casually parading by, mostly in double file, were Clifton, Daryl, Cookie, Shawn, Lester, Peete, Charley, Chauncey, and finally Curtiss. My heart started racing like crazy. I took a couple of deep breaths and said, "Hi, Curtiss!" Where did that ditzy dame voice come from? I sounded like Nell Carter squeezed into a two-size, too-small girdle.

He looked down at me with those mirror shades on and said, "What's up?" That deep voice of his made me quiver.

I had my beaming smile on. With me, there are four phases to my smile: bashful, sensual, sexy, and then beaming. I had intended on using my sensual smile but my adrenaline was out of control.

I finally got around to telling Curtiss nothing was happening and asked if he was busy that night. Curtiss leaned forward, looking like he was inspecting me for zits, and asked if I was feeling okay. I said, "Just great!"

"Then how come you're talking like that?" he asked.

"Like what?" I said trying to play it off.

"Like an airhead," Curtiss said.

I was so embarrassed I froze. If I could've found the nerve, I would've turned my back and walked away. Here was the best opportunity of my life to hit on the sharpest man since Billy Dee Williams, and I come across like Laugh-In's Goldie Hawn. In those moments, with Curtiss staring at me through those blind sunglasses, I discovered what was meant by eternity standing still.

Then Kent came by. "Hey, Curt!" he interrupts completely ignoring me, "You going to Taylor's set tonight?"

"Definitely," Curtiss says.

Kent gave Curtiss the brother's shake, and then briefly stared at me as if I were diseased before he moved on.

Curtiss looked down at me for a long second, in his cool, serious way, and says, "You wanna go?"

Just like that, Curtiss asked me if I wanted to go to Taylor's party. I muttered a string of affirmatives like "Yeah -- sure -- okay -- uh-huh."

"Chill out," Curtiss says and puts his hands on my shoulders. I almost fainted. "Give me your address. I'll pick you up at eight."

He hands me a pen and one of his notebooks, the one with RUN DMC on the cover. I wrote down my name, address, zip code, telephone number -- including area code, and best times to call. The man must've thought I was a borderline idiot.

That was our first date.

Curtiss was my first love, my only lover.

I hope, someday, he'll understand why I stayed home.

STORY FOUR

Beneath a weighted canopy of winter's early dusk
-- The Prophet

Evening was cold. School had been canceled the day before due to an anticipated snowstorm. Most of that winter afternoon I had spent participating in tackle football, amid icy snow and subzero temperatures. All able-bodied men in our neighborhood teamed together to create a simple network of wide paths leading from doorstep to sidewalk to the next doorstep throughout the entire block. For us, those passages were avenues of infinite excitement, adventure, mystery, and intrigue. Cowboys and Indians, American soldiers overwhelming a foreign enemy, secret agents thwarting communist spies, thieving pirates on the high seas, explorers seeking treasure in icy caverns harboring creatures unknown. Confrontations were acted out with snow-manufactured weapons: bullets, bombs, arrows, tomahawks, cannonballs, knives, bayonets, and grenades.

"You're dead."

"Am not."

"Are too."

"Am not. You only wounded me."

"That was a grenade. It blew up your whole body."

"Did not!"

"Did so!"

"It only took off one arm. I can still fight. I got another one."

"You'd probably bleed to death trying to fight with one arm."

"I would not!"

"You would so!"

On and on we created new scenarios of good versus evil. Worlds where justice always managed to eke out a triumph. Then the inevitable occurred. Our favorite winter pastime would joyfully emerge from the mere suggestion that we play: football. The word breathed into us unanimous glee. Slipping, stumbling, tripping, sliding, belly flopping and pratfalls on slick, child-made, dull gray carpets where once lay thick pads of fresh white snow, we proceeded to horribly emulate those sports heroes we idolized. This mockery of sport and vaudeville continued until that fateful moment when the uncompromising voice of Grant's mother loudly ordered Grant inside. With Grant went the football.

We persevered by sculpting footballs out of snow. It didn't work of course. After whoever had, the snow-football was tackled -- if they didn't simply fall on it, drop, or crush it -- new imitation pigskins were constructed to replace its demolished predecessors. Intense arguments arose about how they should be designed. No one knew the actual dimensions of a real football (not that that would have mattered). No one had ever seen a real football, which I would later discover was twice as large as the one Grant owned. Size, shape, and weight became important issues needing accurate answers, matters to be hatched out and decided upon by a committee to maintain correctness and ensure the sanctity of our most beloved game. Once these points were hammered out to majority satisfaction, another instrument of play would be crafted. With each new ball sprang up novel considerations. To pass or not to pass, should the ball be hiked (particularly since it had a tendency to fracture or crumble during the exchange)? Should the person who had the football originally keep it for the entire play? What about lateraling -- or as we put it, throwing the ball backwards? How did we know when there was a fumble?

Each of us had our own preferences. Toby for instance was marshaled against passing, no surprise there. Toby couldn't catch Grant's football without it bouncing off his face. Curt wanted the ball rounder like a fat snowball. He was quickly vetoed. Had we been playing baseball or basketball, it would have been a valid suggestion. In football, it was definitely out of the question. Independently, each proposal was raised, voted on, then instituted or rejected. Former agreements were abolished after one play and reinstituted later. No snow football lay wrecked without having existed under its unique set of conventions.

After each play, something else occurred besides the structuring of a new football. Reggie brought it up first when he said he could not feel his toes. As if that statement touched us like an electric shock, we all suddenly realized, that along with our toes, parts of our own person could not be felt as well. Fingers, cheeks, noses, ears and the less believable eyelids, elbows, knees, and butts joined a list of numb parts. Eventually, Curt made the courageous suggestion that we quit. With mild reluctance, we all agreed. Parting with a few random snowballs bursting near their marks, we miniature-frozen athletes walked our separate ways home beneath a weighted canopy of winter's early dusk.

Mom immediately ushered me into my bedroom where she systematically stripped me of my wet hat, coat, pants, scarf, socks, sneakers, briefs, and thermal undershirt in exchange for a dry pair of loose-fitting cotton shorts, all the while chiding me on my critical foolishness at remaining outside in dangerously cold weather for so long. (Especially since I was supposed to be home by two that afternoon, a fact she had either dismissed or forgotten.) In all honesty, I did not know -- at that age -- winter weather such as that could turn a person's lungs to ice, freeze one's blood, or inflict a degree of frostbite so destructive it could result in the loss of fingers and toes. I was having fun with my equally foolish playmates. That was all I was aware of on that wintry day.

Cradled in her arms, bunched up against my mother's ample bosom, shivering and feeling safe, I was carried into the bathroom where she placed me standing inside the bathtub and ran lukewarm water over my hands and feet, fussing all the while. "What about my nose?" I asked. Mom flicked a few harmless drops of water at my face. They made me flinch. Mom laughed.

Mom continued to fuss and things went perfectly fine. "Gratey, sometimes I believe you're absent the plain good sense God gave most children. How could you not realize when you can't feel something -- things you were feeling before -- that something wasn't right?" Mom asked me this question in all earnest as if she expected a competent response. I said nothing. Her hands worked diligently, rubbing my hands under the water.

"Don't you know better than to stay out in weather this cold?" When mom looked directly into my face that was my cue: "I don't know."

"What do you mean you don't know?" hesitating momentarily after she asked. Not really expecting me to say anything before continuing to fuss and rub.

It was not long before I started feeling what felt like thousands of tiny needles in my fingers and toes. "Mom, my fingers hurt my toes too. Feel like things are sticking them."

"That's good pain honey, means they're coming back to life." Then she went back to fussing. "Maybe next time you'll come home 'stead of staying out in the cold like you crazy."

"Yes ma'am." I listened, apologized, agreed, and then listened some more, all the time enjoying her brisk rubdown of my hands, feet, arms, legs, and occasional brush across my nose and cheeks. I savored the deep tones of concern and mellifluous melody of her voice: "Gratey, Gratey, Gratey. Baby what am I going to do with you?" Had I known how to express the feeling I had at that moment, I would have told her to love me, mom. "I don't know mom," is what I said.

"Can you feel your fingers, your toes? Is that better?" I nodded a deaf yes to each question. "They're coming back to life." I smiled at her. "What you grinning at?" She had caught my smile on her face. I surprised her with a hard hug around the neck. What motivated me to do it? I don't know. Something leaped up inside me. Guess you could say it was love but it felt different, akin to love in its warmth and depth of closeness and feeling. All that stuff we harbor for those few choice people in our lives. Whatever it was, it bubbled up in me so fast and furious I had to let it out right then and there. Mom let me hug her for a while, her arms firm about my thin frame. She smelled great, like cocoa butter. Her skin was softer than my pillows. I closed my eyes and enjoyed her embrace.

With stark suddenness mom went back to fussing: "Boy if you don't get your clammy hands off me, I'm going drown you!" But she was laughing, still hugging me back. I knew she didn't really mean for me to let go. If she had, she would have tickled me under my armpits. When she finally did tickle me, some time after her affectionate threat, I let her resume bringing my deceased limbs back to life.

The needles stopped. I told mom so. She dried me from neck to toes and told me to stand in front of a heater after I ate.

Before I did as instructed, mom led me by the hand back to my room and handed me another pair of baggy white shorts and a short-sleeved green shirt. "Dinner is on the table," she said as she hurried off to her room to change out of her "wet things."

Two friends of my parents, Roz and Woodrow, sat in our living room on our puffy couch directly across from the living room gas heater. They were there when I got home. I knew I was not supposed to be in the living room when my parents had guests, but I would conveniently forget that rule -- selective amnesia that would later serve my purpose.

Mom and her friends were waiting on my father to come home from work so they could begin their all-night marathon of bid whist. Once dad arrived, first he would eat. (His dinner of meatloaf, mashed potatoes, and green peas were kept warm in the oven). Then he would set up the card table and chairs in the den (aided by Woodrow). After dad made certain everyone had what they wanted, he would mix himself a Canadian Club and Squirt on the rocks, marking the prelude to a night of drinking, joking, eating, laughing, card playing, and harmless badgering.

I quickly dressed; skipped into the dining room where I plopped down in my usual chair and preceded to wolf down hot, homemade chicken noodle soup that I assumed had been warmed for me by my mom. Had I known Roz did it as a favor to mom; I would not have eaten it. When I finished, I carefully carried the empty bowl and soupspoon to the kitchen, where on tiptoe and with some measure of concentrated effort, I managed to place them safely in the sink.

Had circumstances been different, mom would have dragged me by my ear if necessary, into my own room when I innocently positioned myself in front of the living room gas heater. After all, she never specified which heater. Her look told me she disapproved of my being there, but would allow me to stay, that time.

Mom was thin and had a lot less aches and pains then. (This was before the invasion of varicose veins, chronic back problems, and bad feet). But on that evening, it was her dark brown eyes suspended in a damp embrace, coupled with a smile that dissolved my few worldly doubts that dominate my recollection of her.

Waves of dry heat massaged the bare backs of my resuscitated legs as I stood before the gas heater, hands behind my back, thawing out the rest of the way. They laughed, talked, and sipped hot tea as I watched, a six-year-old observer with a grin. They seemed not to mind. Quiet me only speaking when spoken to.

Roz was much shorter than mom. I remember Roz as being round: round face, hands, butt, shoulders, and belly. Dad did not care much for Roz, although he tolerated her because she was mom's best friend. I did not like her either. Her smile was a lie her eyes never told. Eyes that were sharp and carnivorous. They made me uneasy when we were alone and Roz would stare at me calling me to her with her lying smile. I never came to her. I did not like Roz at all.

Woodrow was dad's best friend. He was wide and square and had large hands. His eyes constantly gleamed, like sunlight through clear glass. And he had a laugh that was heartier than any Santa Claus I had ever heard. He always wore tan leatherwork boots and had white whiskers and a pinch of snuff tucked inside his bottom lip. His bass voice made me smile, though there were times his breath would stink and I could not understand what he was saying.

When dad got home, the evening was set in motion. Sometime between the first hand of bid whist and my dad telling everyone this marvelous story about when he was eleven and first went hunting with his father, I fell asleep.

In the morning, my internal alarm clock woke me in time to enjoy Saturday morning cartoons. To get to the living room, where the solitary television in the house resided, I had to tiptoe past my parents' bedroom. I overheard sounds: grunting, groaning, moaning, bedsprings squeaking. I had heard these sounds emanate from my parents' bedroom before. Later in life, I would discover those noises to be the music of lovemaking. It is difficult to say for certain since that music was made frequently by my parents, but, I believe, in those early winter hours on one of the coldest days ever experienced in Pittsburgh, Camille was conceived.

STORY FIVE

Casting his net upon tainted waters
-- Ai Quoc Nguyen

There he is again, that crazy black man with his stick, ranting about God and redemption. Doesn't he have anything better to do than to make a fool of himself? Why don't the police cart him away to a psychiatric care facility? Perhaps they could help him there. At the very least, it would get him off the streets.

My name is Ai Quoc Nguyen. I work as a personal loan officer at the Bank of America cater-corner to Kaufmann's. I have been with the Bank of America for eighteen months. In that time, almost every working day, I have seen that lunatic preacher lift up his voice through all sorts of weather and harassment casting his net upon tainted waters. I will say this much for him, he may be insane but he has fortitude, commitment, and determination. I admire those qualities in anyone. Qualities I am personally acquainted with.

My parents fled Central Vietnam for America well before the American military became involved in what was up until then a civil war. Both my parents worked hard to give my brothers, sisters, and me a decent life. We inherited a hard work ethic from them. You could say our family is an American success story. A tale that is sometimes hollow in its center.

The dominant culture has not accepted but only tolerated us. Stereotypes persist. We are appreciated for our exotic cooking and "fascinating" culture. My people are lumped in with other groups of Asians as having some innate engineering or scientific prowess. The detrimental side of those characterizations, besides their not being true, is that our other abilities are often overlooked. We are merely people, human beings as diverse and dispersed in personalities, capabilities, and talents as any other. There is difficulty getting some people to recognize that in us. Stereotypes are easier to digest.

I was born in this country; conceived on U.S. soil. I am a second-generation Vietnamese-American, educated and indoctrinated as an American, fully aware of my Vietnamese culture and history. While I fluently speak, read, and write the tongue of my ancestors, I am equally adept at English. I speak perfect English and possess a Master's Degree in Business Finance from Carnegie Mellon University. I look the part of the loan officer: suit, tie, polished shoes, well groomed -- no different from any of my colleagues. Still, the initial reaction far too often from many of my non-Asian compatriots is to treat me like a foreigner. I am often spoken to in a slow, deliberate fashion as if I were mentally challenged. My way of attempting to short-circuit that perception is to speak first whenever possible. That always sets the person straight as to what they can expect from me. It doesn't stop unenlightened people from displaying their ignorance by saying things such as: "You speak English better than me. Where are you from?" When I tell them Pittsburgh, they are usually stumped. Only the bold ask, "No, I mean originally?" When I affirm I was born and bred in Pittsburgh, they eventually give in. After all, you would not want to upset the person responsible for overseeing the approval of your personal loan.

Then there are the racists, the people who despise me for being Vietnamese. To some, I am taking the food out of the mouths of more deserving Americans. That's right-wing lingo for white. To others, I symbolize the first American defeat in a major conflict. My people tarnished the U.S. war record. My record as well, I suppose. Those same people seem capable of disregarding the fact that the biggest casualties sustained due to the Vietnam conflict were not American GIs -- some of whom were Vietnamese -- but the Vietnamese people. A unified Socialist Republic of Vietnam has only existed since 1976. My fatherland is still trying to heal and find its way in this modern world.

Acceptance is possibly my biggest challenge as an American. Being acknowledged for whom I am and not some fabricated preconception. This is usually not as a Vietnamese-American as I see myself. In that regard, I feel like the strange man who rants on the corner. I want to yell, kick, and scream for someone to recognize me as a human being. No different from any other flesh and blood and bone ignited by a soul.

I love my family. I love who I am. I am proud to be Vietnamese American. I have been repeatedly asked why I cannot simply call myself American. When the time comes when I can be fully accepted and respected as an American, when my culture is welcomed as a full serving on Old Glory's menu, then I will include myself as solely American. Until that time, my race will precede my nationality.

My parents have repeatedly told us about our grandparents. Of my grandparents, only my paternal grandmother is still alive. None of my brothers or sisters have visited our surviving grandmother. When we were younger, my parents would visit her in South Vietnam. They refused to take any of their children with them. They told us it was too expensive. I believe my parents were afraid. I believe they harbored a fear of being trapped in Vietnam with no way out. They kept us in the U.S. to make certain -- if that were their fate -- it would not be ours. I am the only one of my parents' children to take it upon myself to visit Nguyen Le Xuan, my grandmother, the woman who was a legend in my mind. Through her eyes, what I discovered was that nothing could prepare anyone for war.

With my parents' reservations and blessings, I visited my relatives in South Vietnam. I met uncles, aunts, cousins, nieces, and nephews from Quan Long to Thanh Hoa. Many were old enough to have gone through the Vietnam War. Each of them had war stories to tell. I found them interesting and heartbreaking. None was more so than my grandmother's story.

Her presence was so affable that my nervousness upon meeting my grandmother quickly dissolved. She was living with my Uncle Minh in Da Nang. My Uncle Minh owned a number of businesses in South Vietnam and the Philippines. The house we were in had twenty rooms, all but one handsomely furnished in modern South Vietnamese decor. It was only one of a number of homes my uncle owned throughout the world, including one in the United States.

After a wonderful family dinner, we were having tea in the dining room. Earlier that evening my grandmother had made light of my American sounding Vietnamese. The family chimed in with other such comments dispersed between compliments of pride and reminders of duty to our family and our people. My grandmother asked if I alone would escort her to her room. In our culture, what is sometimes stated by our elders as a request is often an implicit command. Of course, I escorted my grandmother to her room as she asked, and did so with honor.

Her room was the smallest in my uncle's large house that looked out over the South China Sea to the west and the sprawling city landscape to the east. We could see Uncle Minh's mid-sized shipyard along the western shore from where we stood. The salt sea breezes were brief but welcomed. It was early summer and the tropical heat and humidity of Da Nang was beginning to make its presence felt. My grandmother had insisted on a small room with modest furnishings, one she could maintain herself. As the only surviving parent of my father's parents, we honor and respect her as an elder and revere her for her gift of survival.

My grandmother wore traditional clothing: a brilliantly embroidered, high-necked, long-sleeved red dress with front and back panels worn over white satin trousers. Her long silver hair was wound into a tight bun held in place by two ornate white chopsticks. Time had been unkind to the face and petite body of my grandmother. After hearing her story, I understood how her experiences contributed to her frail appearance. I also came to understand that she had an immense spirit and a great heart.

"Your Uncle Minh has done well for himself," my grandmother said. She spoke in Vietnamese as she did the entire time of my visit. Not because she could not speak English, she simply refused.

"Yes grandmother," I said in my American accented Vietnamese.

"As have all of my children, I am very fortunate indeed."

"And I much more to have a grandmother such as you," I said.

She smiled. "You pay me too much homage Ai Quoc. Save it for when I am dead."

"Let us hope that day is far from now."

"I have seen much. When the day comes for me to join your grandfather, I am ready."

I respectfully nodded not knowing what to say.

"Only I am left to tell my story," my grandmother began ending our brief silence. "In 1923, the Year of the Boar, I was born to Duong Khac Ly and Chan Thi Hoa, sandwiched between three sisters and three brothers, all of whom have passed on, your great-aunts and uncles. Do you show the proper respect to your ancestors Ai Quoc?"

My grandmother stared at me. It was a warm look, firm and steady, one impossible not to mistake for affection. I respectfully nodded. "I always revere my ancestors, grandmother," I said.

"It is good you have chosen to honor some of our customs," she said emphasizing her statement with a knowing nod before gazing back out over the horizon. I knew that was a reference to my being Catholic. At the time, I thought if I were fortunate, it would end there. I was not.

"We lived in a modest farm village called Hieu Duc. We were simple peasant farmers then as we are now. That simple life remains in our hearts if no longer in our pockets."

My grandmother was referring to the economic good fortune with which our immediate family had been blessed. We have family in the U.S., the Philippines, Hong Kong, and South Vietnam. Most of us are middle class to mildly wealthy. Our hard work ethic has been the cornerstone of it all, that and a little luck. I noticed my grandmother looked at me from the corners of her eyes. She was checking to see if I understood. I acknowledged I did with a humble smile. She continued.

"I was a school teacher. We were peasants blessed with the means to educate our children. Devout Buddhists in faith, loyal to our teachings, dedicated to the Four Noble Truths and the Eightfold Path. Are you familiar with Buddhism, Ai Quoc?"

"Yes grandmother," I answered.

"You are a Catholic?" my grandmother asked. Because of my faith, I am viewed by some of my people as being a banana, yellow on the outside and white on the inside. I briefly wondered if my grandmother now regarded me as such. I could only nod.

"Is that true of the rest of my son's American family?" To this, my grandmother already knew the answer. Out of respect, I played along even though I was hurt by her use of the word American. She had meant it in a derisive backhanded way. It was the only time I can ever recall having been ashamed of being an American. I explained to my grandmother that in addition to me, my mother and my sisters, Ngo Huong and Ti Trang, as well as my brother, Tan Kim, were practicing Catholics. I did not mention to her that I had been an altar boy and at one time considered entering the priesthood. This, too, she may have already known. The rest of our family embraced Buddhism, I concluded. She smiled an enchanting smile for such a wise old woman.

"Your father has remained true to himself. There is something to be learned from that Ai Quoc."

I nodded respectfully.

"Are there many Buddhists in America?" she asked.

"There are some. Their numbers are steadily increasing."

"That is good, very good. Perhaps one day soon one more will be added to their order."

"Yes grandmother," I said trouncing what I was thinking, which was, that one more would not be me.

"Did you know your mother's father was a Buddhist monk?"

I nodded.

"Lap An Tung. He set himself on fire in protest against President Ngo Dinh Diem's mistreatment of Buddhists."

"Mother has told me, grandmother."

"President Diem was a Catholic."

"Yes grandmother." There was a deliberate pause.

"You must follow your heart, Ai Quoc, wherever it may lead you."

There was silence. I waited, as did she. Words are often the least effective means of communication. What is said about silence is true. It can speak volumes. My grandmother had made her point.

"It was in the Buddhist temple of our village your grandfather and I were wed, a modest affair -- particularly by today's lavish standards. But no less joyful." She turned to look at me for a moment. "He was a very handsome man that Nguyen Hung Nghia, much like you, Ai Quoc, strong and fearless, like a tiger. Smart like your father in matters of the world. I must admit, however, in matters of women he was like most men, not very insightful. Yet I loved him, mostly for his big heart. He loved as no other I have known before or since, with an open and honest affection that would have made most women jealous but not me. Why, you may ask? Because I realized it was only me he wanted in the way that men desire women. He reserved that sacred love for me alone. I ask you, what woman could ask for more from her husband?"

I had no answer. She did not expect one.

"You are not yet married Ai Quoc?"

"No grandmother."

"Any prospects?"

"No grandmother."

"Then I should not expect great-grandchildren from you any time soon?"

"No grandmother."

She sighed. "Pity."

The story came unexpectedly from her like a sudden cough. Her mood became somber. Her head rose a little higher. She gazed at the bright red sun on a limpid horizon.

"War has been a constant nemesis to the Vietnamese people. Ever since I can remember, there has been turmoil in our country. It is something I have borne witness to since I was a little girl. We have fought the Chinese, the Japanese, the French, the Americans, and eventually each other. All we wanted was our freedom and our land. Communism did not offer us those pearls as far as our village was concerned, only another master to serve. Being a peasant farmer is a difficult life but it was ours. We were at peace in that modest village of Hieu Duc. We felt many blessings for it being so for we were not blind or deaf to what was happening in our country. It was the Year of the Horse. 1954. That was the year we sent your parents away.

"Before the defeat of the French colonists, Vietnam was one country. My father, and your grandfather's father, fought in that struggle for our nation's independence just as your great-grandfathers fought the Japanese. We were not Viet Cong mind you. Let us simply say we were starving. Our freedom was the food we craved. Since it was not offered, we took it.

"After the imperialists were defeated Vietnam became divided. We in the South became known as the Republic of Vietnam espousing democratic ideologies be that what they may. Ho Chi Minh had proclaimed the North as the Democratic Republic of Vietnam after the Japanese surrendered. I had always found the word "Democratic" in reference to the North a rather ironic joke. Do you imagine Ho Chi Minh had that same thought Ai Quoc?"

"I do not know grandmother," I said in all earnestness, amused by the idea.

"Make no mistake, Ho Chi Minh and the Viet Minh helped liberate us from the imperialists. We are now an independent nation because of those valiant efforts. We have problems, but they are our problems to resolve; our way."

My grandmother waited a moment before she spoke again. Perhaps allowing her statement to ferment in my mind long enough to take back to America with me.

"Our village received word that President Diem had Hieu Duc targeted for the Strategic Hamlet Program. Do you know what that is?"

"Vaguely grandmother," I said.

"For us it was the equivalent of a forced labor camp. There was much discussion amongst the men whether to peacefully resist or use force; even joining the Viet Cong sounded feasible at the time. One decision was made immediately. It was time to free some of our children from our country's hostile fate. We were peasants. We had little money. Everyone agreed that one member from each family would be awarded passage upon a ship bound for the Philippines. From there they could find passage to America. A parent can make no more painful choice than to decide on which of their children to bestow the wings of freedom. Your grandfather and I asked for guidance from deep within ourselves. We asked our ancestors to choose for us. So you see, Ai Quoc, you have your great ancestors to thank for your good fortune as well. We merely did their bidding."

"I am eternally grateful to you as well as my ancestors, grandmother."

"We are a very proud and resilient people, Ai Quoc, steeped in tradition, rich in culture, ferocious in spirit. That was something the Chinese, Japanese, and French did not understand. Neither did the Americans. Do you?"

"Yes grandmother," I answered. She stared at me. I stared back. *Using my tears for ink, I turn my thoughts into verses*, I thought. Where those words came from, I do not know. At that moment, that was what I saw in the ancient eyes of my grandmother. Without a word, she gazed back at the horizon. I did the same. After a long sigh she said, "It is always easiest to tell a story after the dust of turmoil has settled. Then the facts and emotions stand tall in clear view. I see it now as if it were yesterday.

"It was the rainy season. My tears were washed away in the rain. Our village received word that a Buddhist monk had set himself on fire in Saigon earlier that week in protest to President Diem's treatment of Buddhists. He had been the fifth holy man to do so in as many weeks. Trouble was in the wind. The Viet Cong had wasted little time after the imperialists' defeat. Their guerrilla war night strikes on the South and communist propaganda were constant nuisances. The signs were all there. A full-scale civil war would soon begin, which was why your grandfather and I were able to let your father go so easily. We did not want our children swept up in the apocalyptic wave of revolution.

"Your father was but eighteen when we sent him on his journey. Already your father had taken a bride. Lap Cam Hoa, your mother, was but sixteen. We arranged with her family so that she could join your father.

"Neither of your parents wanted to leave. It made them sad to desert their homes, their families. Being their parents, we knew best.

"We gave your parents all of the money we had, some food, and a few clothes. My special gift to your father was a small pouch of soil from my personal garden. A bit sentimental, I know. It made us both feel better at the time."

"He still cherishes it grandmother."

"As I do him; we also gave our children our family stories so that they could pass along their heritage to their children."

My parents had done an excellent job in passing along my grandmother's stories. Ever since I can remember, they regaled us with our history and our heritage, adding to them their own stories. I did not interrupt my grandmother to tell her this. It would have been disrespectful and not to mention unnecessary.

"I did not travel those final miles to Da Nang with my son to see him off on his journey. He shared that trip mostly with his father. 'The rain fell like liquid sunshine on our children as they stood upon the deck of the ship when it left our shores.' My husband described it as such: 'You would have been proud of Duc Thang, Le Xuan. Our son left with dignity just as we taught him.' Your grandfather demonstrated. 'He stood tall like a soldier at attention, nobly waving one hand in the air. Cam Hoa cried. Much of the time, her face was pressed to Duc Thang's chest. But our son did not shed one tear. He is a man, Le Xuan. He will do well in America.' I could see how your father looked from your grandfather's excellent reenactment. When your grandfather finished, he broke down and cried. Together we baptized our child's departure from our lives with tears."

"Although I have seen your father many times since then, it is a trek I wish I had taken. To watch him board that ship that took him to the Philippines en route to America, to wave farewell from the shore, a moment lost I still regret. But then who would have cared for our family, or our farm, if I had gone with them? Practical, no?"

Her voice momentarily betrayed her. There was remorse in her last words. "Yes grandmother," I said. "It was a very practical decision."

"I prayed in the temple on the morning your father and mother left. It was important to me to ask our ancestors to look after your parents from sacred ground, a place from which my voice could be clearly heard by our forbearers. What was truly memorable about that moment was, when I began my prayer there were but a few of us. By the time I finished, the temple overflowed with villagers who were doing the same. With our collective voices reaching out to our ancestors, how could they not hear us? We were fortunate. All of the children we sent found safe passage out of Vietnam. Their beloved escorts returned to us unharmed. Our prayers were answered."

"My parents attend a reunion in honor of that day every year in San Francisco," I said. "They call it the Hieu Duc Village Freedom Celebration. Do you know about that grandmother?" I was looking to please my grandmother in some way. Being the first to bring her such news would certainly have done just that.

"I do Ai Quoc. Your father has told me of such a celebration. It was wonderful news. Has he mentioned my request to you?"

"I'm not certain grandmother," I said. "Which request might that be?"

"The one asking if one day the children of Hieu Duc village would hold their reunion on their native soil."

"He has said nothing to me about it grandmother."

"Perhaps he's still giving it some thought."

"I'm certain father is doing everything he can grandmother."

"Let us hope he will find success Ai Quoc." Without pause, she continued her story. "It was not until 1962, in the Year of the Tiger, that we were forced into a strategic hamlet. A little more than eight years after your parents had left us. The South was at war with the North. President Diem's hamlets were supposed to be for our own benefit to protect us from any possible Viet Cong insurgence. We were compressed into much tighter living areas by President Diem's army for reasons we could not understand. We were forced to live inside enclosed bamboo fences and thatched homes, all of which we had to construct ourselves. There were not enough materials available to build homes for everyone. Close to six thousand of our people were forced to abandon their crops, compelling them to work for others to survive. Hundreds of our young men were carted off for consignment in the South Vietnamese army. Our traditions were not respected. Our ancestral burial sights totally ignored. Our temple was destroyed, replaced in our compound with a Catholic church. Assimilation was clearly part of President Diem's plan. Of course, we did not comply.

"From the devastation of our lives, we were expected to learn about civic duties. A concept we obviously had a much clearer understanding of than our president. From us, they usurped our freedom and in return, they expected obedience and gratitude. We plowed, planted, and harvested no longer for ourselves but for Diem's regime. Call it what you will, but it was forced labor. It was painfully clear to all of us that we were not participants in our civil war, only victims of it.

"Far too often the South Vietnamese army behaved like the Viet Cong they were supposed to be protecting us from. No one was allowed to leave or enter the hamlet without clearance from the army commander. Anyone caught sneaking in or out were considered Viet Cong collaborators. Punishment was either execution or being deported to a detention center for reeducation. To be accused was a guaranteed sentence. Most sentences resulted in execution. Of these unjust killings I witnessed far too many. The accused were forced to kneel. They were then shot through the back of the head. I will not tell you any more of the horrors I bore witness or the humiliation I was subjected to under the watchful eyes of the South Vietnamese army. Let us simply say, perhaps that old adage is true: Absolute power corrupts absolutely."

"In November of 1963, in the Year of the Rabbit, President Ngo Dinh Diem was overthrown and then assassinated by General Duong Van Minh. General Minh's reign was short-lived. He was overthrown and assassinated by General Nguyen Khanh. The South Vietnamese soldiers guarding us received new orders from General Khanh. They abandoned us to fight against the Viet Cong near Hue. We wasted no time tearing down their fences and spreading out onto our land.

"Not long after General Khanh was in power, the Americans became fully involved in our war. We had seen little of the Viet Cong but had heard enough trustworthy reports of their activities to realize this meant the worst sort of trouble. The Viet Cong were merciless against any they regarded as their enemy. All who were not communists were considered enemies of the state, enemies of the Viet Minh. If you were fortunate, you would be sent to a reeducation camp. If you were not, you were tortured and often murdered.

"The Viet Cong attacked our village one night, quick and lethal and as merciless as their reputation, indiscriminately murdering children, women, and the elderly as if they were diseased animals to be slaughtered. I lost Pin Hy and Phuoc Gan on that tragic night. My beautiful sons sought the highest bliss, nirvana. They were older brothers of your father. Pin Hy and Phuoc Gan had deserted the South Vietnamese army after President Diem had arrested, tortured and killed thousands of Buddhists in Saigon. We were so pleased to have our sons home. Your grandfather was so enraged at our sons' deaths he was ready to single-handedly take after the Viet Cong. Family and friends were able to restrain him, calm him down, before he did anything foolish.

"The next day, we buried our dead and said our final goodbyes. It was truly the saddest moment of my life. The Viet Cong insurgence into our province forced many of us to flee to nearby Da Nang. It was the last I saw of my village. What remained of our family stayed together. It is here we began making a new life for ourselves. We have survived to fight another war."

There were tears on my grandmother's cheek. She quickly wiped them away. I pretended not to notice.

"For years our embattled countrymen have fought over ideologies," my grandmother said. "So many dishonorable deaths, so much useless destruction, I can relay to you a good many atrocities I have witnessed and experienced because of war. Why burden your spirit with my nightmares. What I hope -- no, what I pray -- is that no one else will ever endure such barbarism again, especially the sons and daughters of the Vietnamese people. We have suffered enough. Let us forever know peace."

"I add my prayers to yours grandmother."

"There is much more to tell, I grant you this. But that is my story -- how do Americans say -- in a nutshell?"

"You are correct grandmother. That is precisely how the expression goes."

"Now you have my story to add to all the others of our family. Your family is one to be proud of Ai Quoc."

"I am very proud grandmother." She nodded in affirmation.

"Your father has asked me to come live with him in the United States. Would you like that?"

"Very much grandmother," I said with genuine enthusiasm.

"It is enough for me to know of your joy over such a prospect. Vietnam is my home. Here my ashes will be scattered to the winds."

My grandmother paused. Her head had fallen toward her chest. She lifted it toward the sun. "Will you join me in that celebration?"

"With honor grandmother," I said saddened by the thought. She beckoned me to come closer with her forefinger. I bent at the waist positioning my ear near her mouth.

"There is no beginning," she whispered her breath hot on my ear. "There is no end, only the unbroken circle of the universe in all its forms. That is my personal discovery on this journey. Yours may prove different. Accept it or reject it as your heart tells you."

"Yes grandmother," I said straightening. We stood in silence looking out at the South China Sea. My grandmother put a frail arm around my waist. I gently draped an arm over her shoulder. She leaned her head on my shoulder. Her head literally felt as light as a feather. Amazing how time is a conscious invention. It passed rather quickly along smooth stretches of continuous thoughts. Not until sunset did we move.

"There you are Ai," my manager jubilantly said approaching me from behind. My 1:30 appointment Mr. Lathan Davidson accompanied him. I had been standing, staring blankly out of the glass front second floor at the black man still meditating under Kaufmann's clock. For how long I had been there, I was not certain. With a salesperson's smile, I extended my right hand to Mr. Davidson, apologizing for not having been at my desk. My manager had arranged for me to handle Mr. Davidson's prospective account after speaking to him on the phone. This was our first meeting. He gave me that look I recognized. He was taken aback at my race in spite of the fact my name should have told him a good deal about me. That is not unusual. I acquaint it with the difference between seeing and comprehending. You recognize a clear night sky for what it is. Not until you take a moment to observe it are you made aware of its charm. Perhaps that is not the best of metaphors, but I like the connection.

I pointed Mr. Davidson in the direction of our spiral staircase leading down to the first floor where my desk was located, attempting to clear my head of my grandmother's voice as I followed Mr. Davidson down the stairs.

STORY SIX

Eyes as sad as Jesus on the cross
-- Godfrey "Clip" Booke

My name is Godfrey Turner Booke. People call me Clip. I'm a thief.

Why?

Why not?

You got a thing don't you? Work, school, hanging out; mine's the five-finger discount. That's why I'm roaming Gimbel's. Looking to pick up something I can turn into quick cash so I can buy moms a birthday present.

Naw we ain't homeless and we ain't on welfare. Yeah I'm poor. But you don't want to hear that, not in this age of Yuppie Economics. I'm going tell it anyway.

My moms works, now and then, making what she can legally. Mostly she do temp stuff. Sometimes she don't bring home enough dust to make a bill sneeze but she don't quit. I must've gotten the hardhead gene from her.

Try as she may, moms don't understand me. She resorts to well-meant patronizing whenever I do something to get myself in trouble. She can't see that most times what happens is a result of me voicing my opinions or beliefs. Not looking for trouble, but ain't afraid of it either.

Everybody think I'm crazy. Maybe I am. Whatever I do, I'll never be as strange as my pops. Bet he's underneath Kaufmann's clock right now preaching or taking one of his stand-up naps. Yelling at people about repenting and God, shit like that. Moms don't know what's going on with pops. I don't know what set him off but to me he was always strange.

I remember when I was six. He stopped by after he'd vanished for a few years. Moms made the three of us dress up and had us sit and wait on the couch. He came in wearing a suit, clean-shaven, hair neat and trimmed, eyes as sad as Jesus on the cross. He shook Nat's hand, kissed Tehra on the cheek, then squatted down, looked me in the eyes, and brushed my chin with the thumb side of his hooked forefinger. His smile never pierced the sad bubbles of his eyes.

I didn't know anything about Vietnam then. I thought it was us made him feel that way. That's why I never went to see him, although I never told anyone.

He sat across from us and stared. Tehra and Nat and moms tried making conversation with him. Every question was answered with brief, sharp responses or nervous smiles accompanied by downward glances. I didn't say anything. The man made me nervous. All the time he was there, he seemed restless, fidgety, like there was some scary thing lurking around the room only he could see. Whatever made him stay was certainly stronger than that fear.

Moms tried to get me to sit in his lap. I told her straight out, "No!" I didn't say it to be mean. I was just the kind of kid who didn't warm up quickly to strangers. I suppose everybody presumed since he was my father it would not be a problem. Bottom line was I still didn't know him. In time, I would have probably given him all the affection expected of a son toward his pops. Moms understood. I heard her whisper something to that effect to him at the door before he kissed her on the cheek and left never looking back.

Moms suggested we take the initiative and get to know him. Nat was the only one who took her up on it. It must've been worthwhile, 'cause every time Tehra or I'd say something bad about pops, Nat would jump down our throats. For some reason I couldn't bring myself to care. Now it's too late. When I walk by Kaufmann's to say hi or ask how's he's doing, he gives me this long blank stare. And I realize he doesn't even know who I am.

Talking of crazy, I got an older brother and sister. Tehra's the oldest, been saved by Jesus. Thinks I'm second cousin to the anti-Christ. Cool by me. Living in hell may as well be a member of the ruling society.

Big brother's a trip, deals the False White Hope. Everyone outside of family calls him by our last name, Booke. His first name's

Nathaniel. Moms and Tehra and me call him Nat. Most times, I call him other things, things he don't like. He gets pissed off about it. Don't really give a shit. And that I'm told is one of my problems.

It's not that I'm apathetic dig. I simply don't give a good fuck about shit people say I'm supposed to care about.

Take sports: Steelers might make the Super Bowl, I say, so what? What about the AIDS crisis in Africa? Pirates could make the playoffs, I'm thinking, racism and homelessness is on the rise. When I express my constitutionally protected opinion (usually in the middle of something silly like student pep rallies), I'm received with hostile insults and occasional violence. My typical response, since my name ain't Mahatma Gandhi or Martin Luther King, Jr., is tell the pack of wind-head slug-fuckers to kiss my ass. If I'm feeling particularly upset, I'll throw in the word black for good measure. If it ain't happened by then, the last remark usually cost me some body damage.

The sick part is I can't stop. Just can't keep my mouth shut. A prime example is the day Nat picked me up from school.

It was this past May, last semester of high school, and I'm sitting in Principal Watson's office, listening to his pitifully solemn bullshit about how straight A students like me shouldn't have the kind of discipline problems I'm having. Tell it to Freud, baldy, I'm thinking, but I play it chilly.

"What discipline problems sir?" I ask him with the wide-eyed innocence of that kid Webster on television. He brings up my continual confrontations with other students and peep this, "These constant battles with Mr. McClellan."

McClellan was my history and geography teacher. Talk about bad luck. I had him three out of my four years at Salvation. A short, tow-headed, arrogant intellectual who talks at his students in the same demeaning manner I'd imagine William Buckley would address The Junkyard Dog. Most of my classmates found his haughty manner and pedantry intimidating (that is, the ones who weren't trying to assimilate him). To me he wasn't saying shit.

He and Watson led the charge to try to get my mother to agree to let me skip a few grades so I could enter college early. My moms asked me. I said no. I ain't in no rush to be victimized by false promises from a nation that regards my kind and me as subhuman burdens to be tolerated at best. Let the slug-fuckers wait.

That day, McClellan was talking about Lincoln and the Civil War supposedly giving us the inside story on how it really was.

I'm chilly when he said Lincoln freed the slaves because he detested the institution. I know a little about the man. Read a few books on him. True, Lincoln did detest slavery, but he believed that in an independent democracy, slavery would run its course and die a natural death.

McClellan kept pressing about how slavery was the reason for the Civil War. I'm paying attention as if it was the first time I'd heard the shit. Like I said, I was chillin'.

McClellan asked me if I agreed with his assertion of why Lincoln freed the slaves.

I paused. Now I'm pondering, should I concur or should I give him the word? I decided to elaborate.

I stood up (that was required when answering a question in his class), looked around the room for a second, and then respectfully gave him my answer. "The Civil War was the result of the South's attempts to sever themselves from the Union and become self-governing. Lincoln would not -- justifiably so -- have that. Slavery was merely the issue used to instigate war."

By the time I finished the room was quiet. You could hear the steady buzz of the white-faced electric clock high on the yellowed plastered wall behind his desk. People's mouths were hanging open and they were staring at me like I was Freddie Crougar or something.

McClellan's jaw was tight. I mean, I thought the man was seriously illin'. His face was all red. His eyes narrowed. I knew I'd fucked up. The man hates to be faced especially by me.

Didn't matter it was different that time. I wasn't trying to look superior that's his game. I was simply answering the question to the best of my ability. Isn't that what school's supposed to be about, performing to the best of your ability, not someone else's expectations. Apparently, McClellan didn't think so.

As usual, he breaks into his little game of discrediting via testing your command of the facts. I stand firm, quote my sources, and correct his slight and gross misinterpretations. Progressively, he loses his composure, starts buggin', gets loud and indignant.

I guess you know by now I'm not the kind of person takes shit from anybody. He set the ground rules. I played the game. Shouldn't have started what he couldn't finish.

Now back to Watson. I told him, "Sir, none of the spats with students were ever started by me. As for Mr. McClellan, he always incites situations he is not intellectually equipped to handle."

"Mr. McClellan said you punched him."

"That's not true sir."

On and on and on, same shit, different day, I must've gotten a hundred sermons by glass-head Watson and always with that paternal tone in his voice. Like his never been poor pale hide could possibly know something about me. What the hell was he doing being principal of a 99.9% black school anyway? For that matter, what was McClellan or Koelsch or Plank or Hints or Vaupel or Popken or the rest of the majority white faculty doing there, charity work?

So Watson goes on to say Mr. McClellan said I pushed him and was yelling at him in class. I tried telling him what really happened. McClellan was the one yelling at me. But did he listen, noooooo. Watson says, "Why would Mr. McClellan lie?"

That's when I blew it. I calmly told Watson, "McClellan's a fucked-up, egotistical, anal-compulsive punk, who ain't got the balls of our dog Casper or the brains of a tit."

He just stared at me through them old-fashioned wire-rimmed glasses, not looking angry or frustrated, more like . . . confused. As if someone he loved had just unexpectedly slapped him.

"I don't understand you," Watson said to himself.

I'm a straight A student. Ain't never made nothing but. That's because of this gift I got. Can remember almost everything I see, especially on a printed page. Makes studying a snap. I never told anyone about it. The less people know the better off you are. Know what I mean.

Anyway, he hits me up with three days suspension, and an immediate meeting with my moms. I shrugged my shoulders and told him, "Whatever."

Suspension was a new one for me. I mean you got to fuck up bad to be suspended from Salvation. Usually you got to get caught fighting or possessing a weapon. Even those aren't guarantees to suspension. Jeff Courtney was being tried for a rape he committed on school property, and the bastard didn't miss a day of school 'til the trial. So I was in deep shit and I knew it. Moms kicked my ass for that one, but back to my brother.

Nat shows up, red 'vette and all, telling Watson our moms was at work and asked him to pick me up. That was true enough but Watson was suspicious. I could tell. He had those probes coming out from the corners of his eyes, but he let me go, with a serious warning not to come back without my moms. Before I can say anything Nat grabs me by the collar and runs me on tiptoe out of the office.

Nat's strong, played football, middle linebacker. They used to call him Backbreaker Booke. If he hadn't been so hot for trouble, no telling how far that talent could've taken him.

Nat starts yanging on about why do I keep getting into trouble at school. I tell him school ain't the trouble. It's simple people like McClellan that's the real problem. He don't want to hear it. Nat told me if I fucked up one more time, he was going to whip my little ass.

I had to shake my head, this drug peddling, ex-jock, ex-con, going give me the lowdown on straightening up. I told him to kiss my ass. (I like that expression. It has unmistakable tonal combinations that force one to recognize contempt, not to mention provoking some memorable reactions).

As expected, Nat starts whipping up on me. I broke away, stopped long enough to rattle off a string of expletive-laced insults from a distance, and then ran. Guess Nat figured it'd be better if he left me alone because he didn't follow -- and my brother don't give up easy.

Check out the silver necklace. That should get me the ducats I need. Let's see who they got watching me. Store dicks are as obvious as Dick Gregory at a skinhead convention.

Malcolm! Well, well. Once again, we do battle. I call him Malcolm because his face reminds me a little of Malcolm X. Sorry to do this to you bro'. Don't take it personally.

Baggy pants make this a breeze. Stole some money out of this store once from the Men's Clothing section, dude left to help one of the other sales clerks and didn't close the cash register. I tipped over, emptied out all the green, and slipped away.

It was fresh, a serious push. Know what I mean. What white boys call a rush. That's why I steal. Not for the need (I sell or give away most of what I take). Naw, for me it's definitely the push. I feel alive when I'm reaching for something, knowing one slip, one miscalculation could mean, got your ass.

Almost got caught a couple of months ago.

I was in Kaufmann's in a bit of a hurry that day. Had a date with this college tender roni named Lesilee. Rushed in, purchased my usual fifty-cent shopping bag, the maroon ones with the capital cursive K's, and set to work.

In quick succession I lifted a couple of shirts, a pair of pants, and since I was right next to sporting goods, some fishing supplies for when me and my homeboy Earl go to the Allegheny to catch them funky catfish. I really wasn't in tune with my surroundings at the time. Like I said, I was in a hurry.

From behind the round rack of fishing poles steps this dude I call Kojak. I mean this dude had the trench coat, baldhead, and lollipop. I see him out of the corner of my eye making his move.

I quick tipped for the elevators just around the corner from where I was operating. This tall babe was standing there waiting for the elevator. On the floor beside her was the same type of shopping bag I had. I stood next to her. She looked down at me. I looked down the hall like I saw something bizarre. She looked in that direction. Quickly I switched bags. She looked back at me. I was still looking down the hall. The elevator came. I kept staring down the hall, my expression becoming more deranged by the second. She picked up what she believed to be her shopping bag and rushed onto the elevator. The elevator was empty. From where I was standing, I could see the elevator console. She pressed "1" and the "DOOR CLOSE" button simultaneously. I needed to make certain the last thing she thought about was looking into that shopping bag. I turned my head mechanically and gave her my most demented stare. She frantically jabbed the "DOOR CLOSE" button until we watched each other disappear.

By then Kojak must've had an all-points bulletin on me. Three store dicks came out of nowhere to arrest my ass.

They take me downstairs and hassle me. When they find I got cash receipts for everything (including the lingerie), they gets real upset but ain't shit they can do but let me go.

I had no need for the stuff they tried busting me with so I left it near a cash register on my way out of the store. Figured the woman would come looking for it. I thought about writing her a thank you note but I didn't want to push my luck.

Kojak warned me if he ever saw me in Kaufmann's again, he was going to arrest me whether I stole anything or not. *Cool*, I thought, *we'll see about that.*

All that month I went to Kaufmann's every day, found that sucker, and stole at least two things. He didn't catch or arrest me. Just my way of saying kiss my ass, Kojak.

Last go 'round for this filcher though. Be eighteen next month. Big time can't stand that ride, time to transfer to a more respectable hobby. Maybe I'll join the CIA become a double agent or some shit.

STORY SEVEN

We may be God's creation but time is the invention of the Devil
-- Demosthenes "Kojak" Nikolaos

I was born and raised in Oklahoma in a small boxcar community, only child to a carpenter and homemaker. We weren't poor but not far from it. My father insisted on working near home. He constantly turned down good-paying jobs that would take him away from his family and the boxcar home he built himself. Most of those job offers came from neighboring cities. My father refused to move his family into what he would often refer to as "those dens of iniquity."

My father wasn't an overly religious man, but his faith was strong. Cities were where he felt the devil did his best work. That left the community to support us. Living in what was essentially a struggling farming town, he had to accept whatever work came his way. Many times, it wasn't carpentry work at all.

A proud soft-spoken man, who only said what needed to be said, and who took care of his own. We had a little farmland so we weren't so bad off. My father did whatever he had to do, without compromising his beliefs, to keep a roof over our heads, food on the table, and clothes on our backs. His love for me was doled out in the same manner as his words, measured and tempered, which prevented us from ever becoming close. As soon as I was old enough, I joined the army. My leaving for boot camp was the only time I ever saw my father shed a tear.

After serving in the Army infantry during the Korean War, I wound up here, in Pittsburgh, Pennsylvania, liked it, and decided to stay, much to my father's chagrin.

Ever since I can remember, all I've ever wanted to be was a police officer. Under the GI Bill, I earned my B.S. in Criminal Justice from the University of Pittsburgh. I went on from there to graduate near the top of my class from the Pittsburgh Police Academy. That was the beginning of my law enforcement career.

I started on the force as a beat cop. I showed a lot of savvy and keen investigative skills out on the streets, so it didn't take long for me to make detective. It was quite a change from taking orders during an investigation to giving them. I adapted quickly. From Bunco, where I was initially assigned as a detective, I moved on to Narcotics and eventually up to Homicide, which was where I thought I wanted to be.

It turned out I didn't care much for Homicide. Most of the work came after the crime had been committed. I knew that going in. It was like that with most police work, seeking to bring the perpetrator of a crime to justice. On the outside looking in, Homicide appeared the most rewarding of all in that area. The most heinous crime a human being can commit is the taking of another life. When a Homicide detective brought in a perp, handcuffed and ready to be served up to Justice, there had to be no better feeling in the world. Being party to that only made me feel as though I was closing the barn door after the farm animals had left. Bunco left me feeling the same. Narcotics, on the other hand, provided me with more gratification. There was a great deal of undercover work being a narc. It was required to do what narcs do best, stopping a criminal act while in progress.

I requested a return to Narcotics. Permission was granted. Provided I headed a new special unit formed to go after the heavy illegal narcotics suppliers in the Pittsburgh area. During my tenure, we managed to reel in a few big fish. I was awarded a few citations and commendations along the way. One of P.P.D.'s finest, so they told me. I was honest, hard working, and fair. Straight Arrow Nickey, some of the boys at the precinct used to call me. Incorruptible and untouchable, made me proud. One bullet ended it all.

It was during a narcotics bust. My team and I had worked an undercover drug operation down at the docks to perfection. We had the goods and the perps sewed up in one neat little package. The bust was going down. I was in pursuit of John Panciarelli, one of the bigwigs behind a fifty-five million dollar heroin and cocaine operation who looked to be getting away. It was night. I had stopped running and ordered Panciarelli to stop or I would shoot. Out of the corner of my eye, I spotted the shooter. He had stepped out from behind a stack of wooden pallets. He fired just as I had pivoted to take aim. In over twenty years on the force, I had never been shot. His bullet caught me square in my hip. Mine ripped through his heart, bigger gun and better aim. That's why I'm here and the shooter's not. A couple of the boys in blue rounded up Panciarelli.

The bullet I took left me permanently disabled. I have a hitch in my get along that worsens every year. The Captain was forced to regulate me to desk duty. I still had the reins over my narcotics team. Running it from a desk wasn't the same. I needed to be out there to get a real feel for things, to take a pulse. I missed the action. Like what I'm experiencing now as a store detective. It's not P.P.D. Narcotics but it'll do. As much as it hurt to give up my dream, it was time to move on. I opted for early retirement. That was over twenty years ago. It seems like only yesterday.

A teenage girl wearing baggy jeans, expensive tennis shoes, a Steelers jersey, and a Steelers cap turned around backwards, lifted a gold chain in the jewelry section. I roam the store orchestrating my staff. I was in the Men's Cologne section when I spotted her. Pritchett wasn't on to her. That's his department this week. I signaled Pritchett by touching my tie, then pointing to the kid with my index finger while rubbing my chin. Pritchett took the hint. He went over and identified himself as a Kaufmann's store detective, then asked the kid to go with him.

Goodman looked over at the action. She was stationed in perfumes. Goodman jerked her head in their direction. It was her way of asking should she assist. I nodded. Goodman moved in a couple of steps behind the kid without her realizing it. The kid got nervous. She looked scared. She turned quickly to run. Before she managed a step, Goodman had her. The kid yelled for them to get off her, protesting the arrest and proclaiming her innocence. She continued to struggle and protested all the way through the swinging doors leading down to the basement where our offices and holding area are located. There she would be searched, read her rights, formally charged, and taken into police custody. Combined with the paperwork, that would take the better part of an hour.

I moved over to the jewelry section to cover for Pritchett. Split up the team of Davis and Swenson in leather goods, having Swenson cover for Goodman in perfumes. It's Friday. Start of the weekend. Shoplifters will be out in force.

That young woman trying on a silver charm bracelet reminds me of my first wife, Effie, twenty-five years ago. Same full brunette hair, dark piercing brown eyes, warm crooked smile. I've been married three times in all. For various reasons none of them lasted. Can't say I really loved Effie, although I did care for her. Ours was more of a marriage of convenience. We were involved. She got pregnant. It was the right thing to do.

For a while, we were comfortable in our relationship. Around the time Eugene, our second child, was three, comfortable had soured into annoyance and boredom. One day I came home from work and Effie and the kids were gone. I'll admit, if it weren't for my children, I wouldn't have bothered to track Effie down except to serve her with divorce papers. As it was, even with my police connections, it took almost a year to find her. She had taken off with a computer nerd who used to be her grade-school sweetheart of all things. Apparently, he still loved her and she him. Effie and I talked it over. They moved back to Pittsburgh. We divorced amicably and I was granted liberal visitation rights to see my kids. Effie and the nerd are still together and very much in love; my kids, Delmetria and Eugene, are all grown-up and doing well on their own.

My second marriage did not conclude nearly as well. Spirit, spontaneity, and an unquenchable lust for new experiences were what I saw in Mary. What she ever saw in a hard-nosed, hard-working detective such as me, I'll never know. Mary and I started out like Tracy and Hepburn. We were fiery, impetuous, and zany. All the emotion and passion that was missing from my first marriage existed in bucketfuls in my second. Except Mary was an alcoholic. It took me two and a half years to accept that. You never want to believe the worst about those close to you. The price of blind love, I suppose. Came home unexpectedly for lunch one day to find Mary passed out on the couch. She was half-dressed, clutching an empty pint of Black Velvet to her bosom. That was what opened my eyes.

I tried everything I could think of to convince Mary to quit. She flat out refused. Mary did not see her drinking as a problem. She enjoyed it too much. One day I got a call from a uniform at a car accident scene. A woman had crossed over into oncoming traffic, plowing head on into a semi. It was Mary. The uniform assured me she didn't feel a thing. From the looks of the accident scene, Mary was intoxicated and passed out behind the wheel. She died immediately.

The accident occurred ten days after I gave Mary a choice. Get help to stop drinking or I wanted a divorce. I can't say how deep my love was for Mary. Until this day, I don't know. What I do know is I miss her. I only wished I could have found a way to help her. God knows I tried. I cried. I mourned. Then I let her go.

They say the third time is a charm. I don't know if that expression was ever intended to apply to marriages. Candice and I certainly gave it a hell of a try, a long-legged, red-haired telecommunications expert with deep-dish dimples and glowing green eyes. One look at her and my heart was lost, or so I thought. Without question, I loved Candice. The only thing I loved more was my job. That was our downfall.

Candice never really got used to me being a police officer especially an undercover cop, even more so a narc.

We were at Steven Shepard's house, one of my narcotics team, celebrating the Yaconetti sting when it came to a head. There had been gunfire. None of our team was hurt. A uniform went down with a shoulder wound. He was all right. Admittedly, I took a couple of chances that could have gotten me shot, even killed. Reflecting on that, of course, led to my telling of other war stories going all the way back to my beat cop days. None of which set well with Candice. Something I didn't realize until much too late.

Candice was unusually quiet on the trip home that night. Her mood did not change by the following morning. That evening Candice gave me an ultimatum. Candice said she couldn't take being married to a cop any longer. Quit the force or she wanted a divorce. It was the equivalent of asking me to cut out my heart or my soul. I tried explaining to her that resigning as a narcotics detective would kill me in a way no bullet ever could. Candice saw it as a choice between her love and my job. After days of unsuccessfully trying to change her mind, I made my decision.

Candice and I had been divorced thirteen months before I was shot. By that time, Candice had already gotten a job transfer to Harrisburg and was completely removed from my life. After our divorce, Candice told me she never wanted to see me again. She said it was too painful. I had to respect that. It didn't prevent me from entertaining the idea of one day trying to get in touch with her. If only to see how she was doing and to let her know I'm OK. One day turned into years. I had learned to live with the void she left in my heart. There was no sense both of us being unhappy in our personal lives. Staying out of her life was the greatest gift I could give her.

Following my premature retirement from the police force, I was offered a number of top dog security positions; tried two before Kaufmann's. I found them boring and stifling. Most of them involved watching surveillance monitors. Cameras did the majority of the work, security personnel was the response team. There was rarely any action.

I tried private investigative work for a while. It proved to be little more than surveillance work or serving up subpoenas most of the time. At least it allowed me to be mobile. Not cooped up like the security positions I previously held. It still wasn't very satisfying.

Bill Duke was a veteran Bunco detective when I began my career as a police investigator. Bill had taken me under his wing. He retired after thirty years to a position as security chief with Kaufmann's. Bill offered me the job upon his retirement. I took it. I've been working here ever since. Up to this point, that is the sum of my life.

My father was fond of saying, "We may be God's creation but time is the invention of the devil." This philosophical tidbit was usually inspired by a sudden ache or pain he'd recently experienced which he directly attributed to his mounting age. I used to believe it was an awful attempt at humor. My father had a dry wit. At times, it was difficult to distinguish when he was being funny or serious. Now

I believe that with that statement he was expressing both. As far-fetched as it sounded, there may have been a grain of truth in his thinking.

That was only one of the hundreds of things I thought about after my father lost his four-year battle with colon cancer. God rest his soul. Try as I might, I couldn't convince my mother to come live with me. She refused to leave her home. That little farming community had transformed into a modern suburb of pleasing homes and two-car garages. Thanks in the most part to government subsidies paid to residents not to farm the land.

My mother had shared my father's beliefs about cities. So much so that when I would visit home, after a bone-crushing hug and a powerful welcome, she would remind me I was back in God's country, and she expected no less of me than to behave accordingly, which I always did.

Less than two years later, my mother followed my father. His death was too much for her to bear. Mom died of a heart attack, caring for her backyard garden she loved so much. For some odd reason, her passing in that manner allowed me a temporary peace. A tranquility I believe she experienced then, now, and forever.

The death of one's parents is something that cannot be described. There is a throbbing absence layered with unfathomable loss. It is the cruelest law of nature enacted by time, sanctioned by God, a vindictive sentence for an eternal crime. Only the loss of your child outweighs the loss of your parents in your soul. Nothing ever replaces them. It is the rooted conviction they are better off now than they ever were in life that sustains us, makes the unbearable bearable.

Well, well, well, if it isn't Mr. Godfrey Booke. I never forget a face or a name. Paying us another visit, I see. I've been after him for some time. I almost had him a short while back. He gave us the slip, did an old switcheroo on us at the last minute. The stuff in the shopping bag wasn't his. He knew it. I knew it. Every member of my squad present knew it, but we couldn't hold him. There were cash receipts for everything, no signatures. He got lucky. He smiled at me when I told him so. Wise guy, kid was daring me to catch him just like he's been doing ever since.

I actually like Godfrey. The kid has lots of potential. I've done a little background check on him out of curiosity. He has a good home, loving mother, "A" student, college material. His old man skipped out on him when he was a baby, reappeared, then disappeared again. Could explain a few of those behavioral problems his principal mentioned. No rap sheet other than his penchant for the five-finger discount, he's clean.

Most people we catch are poor, no excuse in my book. Kaufmann's doesn't carry what most people need. They carry things most people want. Things most poor people can't afford. Every now and then, you get a kleptomaniac. Poor sick bastards. They really can't help themselves. Too bad, still have to arrest them. It's my job. Godfrey's neither one. In my book, he's a thrill-seeker. He was smug when I tried scaring him straight. This is all a game to him. If I get him behind bars for forty-eight hours, his tune will change.

Snot nose wanted us to call him Clip, like a jug head I asked why. He said it was his nickname. Told me he was a junior barber and then he gave me this wry smile. Smart-ass kid's got a sense of humor. I'll give him that.

There was one trouble spot in his family tree. He has a brother, Nathaniel, drug dealing hard-ass ex-con. I was there when the uniforms brought him in after his failed armed robbery attempt. He was just a teenager but I could tell. He could do the time on his head. Some guys can handle prison. Become as mean as they have to be to survive. I recognized him. Back Breaker they used to call him. Kid was a star. I saw him play a few times. No question in my mind he was pro material, damn shame. You would think Godfrey or Clip or whatever he's calling himself these days would steer clear of crime after what happened to his brother. I could tell from talking to him that the kid's got excellent common sense. His mountain oysters are just a little too big for his own good.

He reminds me of that strange character who parks himself underneath our clock. I had a few run-ins with him when he started. Had some of the boys in blue cart him away on several occasions. No sooner he'd get out he'd be right back on that corner. Now he's like a fixture, a regular landmark attraction. A lot of people who work downtown expect to see that crazy preacher putting on a show. Hell, I've listened to him several times myself. Some of what he says makes sense although there are times when I still find him annoying.

The kid called me Kojak. There is some resemblance to Telly Savalas. I have the baldhead, prominent nose, lollipops, Greek heritage, all coincidence. The trench coat is a carryover from my P.P.D. detective days. Although I'll admit, I got the idea about sucking on lollipops to quit smoking from the show. It worked. I enjoyed the lollipops so much I kept on eating them, replaced my nicotine addiction with a sugar habit. Have to admit, I did like the kid's comparison.

What Mr. Booke does not understand is I make the rules here. The unwritten rule of probable suspicion is all we need to search his person. Using a shopping bag makes searching him just that much easier. He's lucky I'm a fair man. If I listened to my squad and applied the probable suspicion rule, he'd be toast by now. When we catch him, I want it to be with his hand in the cookie jar, so to speak, by the book.

Well, Clip, we'll play your little game of cat and mouse. Today may be your unlucky day. He's spotted me. Good. There's no pretense between us. Goodman and Pritchett are back in position. That leaves me free to roam. Arthritis has set in my hip. It makes it too painful to be on my feet for too long. I'm staring at a desk job again if I stay on. I'm lucky. With my combined pensions and social security, financially, I'll be fine. Don't think I can do the desk jockey thing even at my age. I'd miss the action. Straightening out this Godfrey will be my last good deed before I exit. Question is what do I do after I leave.

STORY EIGHT

An idealistic young man
-- Nikolai Albert Watson

I came to Salvation High School in autumn of 1951. I was an idealistic young man. Philosophically motivated and intellectually armed with a doctorate in education, I was fully prepared to enact a lifetime of altruistic teachings where it was mostly needed.

No matter what race or creed, social status or religion, people are drawn from one common lot: humankind. That acquiescent knowledge was at the heart of my family doctrine, which in essence, enveloped much of what is central to being an American for me. A cherished, momentous gift is how my first-generation Polish grandparents perceived American citizenship. Those who had nothing but believed in themselves could achieve whatever they wished with focused hard work and honest determination. Theirs was the American dream. For some, that dream manifested into fact.

My parents lived according to that dogma and well they should have. After all, they had been fortunate enough to prosper from a lucrative furniture business begun by my father's father, a business that allowed my father and his family (including myself of course) a life without want and brimming with possibilities. What my grandparents and parents believed, I believed as well. Why should Negroes be any different? Why should they not share in the fruits and freedoms of these United States as so many already had?

Understanding that something needed to be done I decided to become a torch lighting a path toward belated redemption. Single-mindedly, I was prepared to aid the Negroes (they weren't called black or African-American then) in their quest for justice and social acceptance. Education was to be my "fresh showers to quench the thirsting flowers." With a full head of thick brown hair, 20-20 eyesight, and the intimidating frame of an offensive lineman, I was granted the opportunity to uplift my outcast brothers and sisters.

In the Pittsburgh educational system, the most undesirable job was principal of Salvation High School. A school populated by "useless, ruthless, shiftless niggers," a school that sent three experienced principals packing in a single academic year. Only a moron would undertake such a task. I wanted that job, and got it, with little resistance, in spite of the fact that I was blatantly unqualified for the position. That's how anxious The Board was to unload it. In retrospect, that same inexperience may have been my largest advantage.

My family and friends thought me insane. A waste of time and talent, they all proclaimed. If any understood my reasoning for doing what had to be done, I was certain my parents would. Even after my extensive explanation detailing the humane reasons I was undertaking such a necessary mission, my parents were convinced I was making a horrible mistake, even though they complimented me on my admirable motives.

It was not my judgments but theirs that were in error. If I could prove that the worst school in the entire city could become academically and behaviorally respectable, then it would set a long overdue precedent, not only for the city of Pittsburgh, but also for the entire country. There are no such things as "useless niggers."

It worked. The first year, I established laws and enforced them with a big stick. Respect for me grew along with apprehension. "What are you doing here?" Students asked me on several occasions. A ridiculous rumor clamored about at one time that I was a spy sent by the Board of Education to gather evidence to close Salvation. It was surprising how many students actually believed that garbage and other such outrageous dribble.

I addressed nonsensical and pertinent issues concerning students at our Monday morning assemblies. These assemblies were my finger on the student body pulse. I could diagnose ailments that might arise that week, out of the normal nest of concerns, and prepare my teaching staff to short-circuit them if possible. It was also an opportunity for students to place their irons in the fire, to voice legitimate frustrations as well as any upbeat experiences they cared to share.

These assemblies always began one hour before classes, so not to steal time away from the most important reason students were there, that of course being to receive an education.

The Monday morning assemblies were also a mandatory part of the curriculum. To graduate, a student had to possess solid classroom and assembly attendance. Assigned auditorium seats simplified tracking students. Not only would a student not graduate without good attendance, he or she would be denied passage to the next grade level as well. If that were not enough, then detention was the next line of punishment, followed by suspension and finally expulsion. All of these methods of discipline were firmly reinforced with tempered physical punishment by my teachers and me when needed. Given the belief that they cared little about education, or society, or even themselves, one might hypothesize a lot of "useless niggers" would revolt against such treatment. Well, they did not. By the first year's end, the majority of Salvation students had grudgingly accepted the newly evoked measures of order.

Things went along smoothly for a while. Students were graduating, prepared mentally (and to some degree socially) to enter American society as contributing adults. Morale was high. Pride was widespread. Salvation became a name spoken with dignity within the community. Those who formerly laughed became intrigued. Distressing as it was, too many of my colleagues honestly believed Negroes were inferior. In proving them wrong, I had focused on education. What I had not estimated in my overall plan was society itself.

Keep in mind that this was a period when segregation was rooted. Negroes were still relegated to riding in the back of streetcars and buses, eating in obscure corners of restaurants and using "COLORED ONLY" bathrooms. Pittsburgh itself had an active Ku Klux Klan membership rivaling any in the south. It should not have surprised me when a number of white parents were not enthralled when Salvation students began winning high school debates, science competitions, math and writing contests, chess tournaments, and the like. Ludicrous claims arose that white students were getting an inferior education. The Board was bombarded with threatening letters and telephone calls demanding something be done about the learning imbalance that obviously existed . . . or else. During one period, not a day went by that the words "nigger lover" wasn't somehow communicated to my staff or me.

On how this problem should be handled, the Board was divided. Some suggested I curb Salvation's inflated education standards. Curtail them just enough to keep students competitive but a bit behind other, coincidentally white, public schools. I angrily denounced that approach, making my feelings clear that my students deserved the same quality of learning as any other child. At one point Wilson Cardinal, then Head of the Board of Education, threatened to dismiss me as principal. After a threat of my own to make the entire racist affair a national scandal, he bitterly abstained from such action, after which, Wilson Cardinal surprisingly stood steadfast by me during the whole insane mess.

Then society decided to alter the way schools did business. Physical discipline was abolished. Although used primarily as a last line of reprimand it proved to be the only measure some students respected. Once word spread that it was unlawful for an employee of the Board to strike a student, certain students became more disruptive. Classes became more difficult to control. Discipline problems increased by scores. I had recruited extraordinary teachers into the fold up until that time. After their hands, and to some degree their tongues became tied, they left for more financially rewarding and less caustic private institutions.

Drugs and alcohol had always been a problem. We were far from unique in that respect. All public and private schools in the city and surrounding districts had the same concern. We, however, seemed in constant competition with three other Allegheny County high schools to see who could escalate it to epidemic proportions. Even with our increased credibility, far too often we led the pack.

Then came the civil rights movement, a substantive injection we sorely needed. Students applied their energies toward civil disobedience, political awareness, and enlightening debates. There was a bristling electricity constantly crackling in the air. Diametric positions evolved between the followers of Dr. King (of whom I was an advocate) and the more militant Malcolm X. Pride and self-worth resurfaced. Teachers who had given up were revitalized. New teachers brought fresh energy and unique prospects. I would rise in the morning stimulated, whistling as I drove to work, greeting students who snarled and smiled at me with equal verve.

Late 60s through the early 70s were a metamorphosis this country had not seen since Reconstruction. Nowhere was it more evident than in the halls and classrooms of Salvation High School. I have never loved my job as much as I did then. I even entertained the attitude that maybe society was right. Perhaps it was time to vanquish the sword.

By the late 70s, I could sense the changing winds. Teenage gangs formed, organized, brutal, cunning, and angry. As with all groups of that nature, they were bullies with a single purpose, to control through intimidation and violence. One element that added fuel to their fire was the high percentage of students who used narcotics. During the peace and civil rights era, the popular drugs were marijuana, barbiturates, amphetamines, LSD, acid, and to lesser degrees, opium and heroin. Then speed became a favorite followed closely by cocaine, designer drugs, and the deadly crack. Gangs became ruthless enforcers of a high school drug cartel, inflicting the sort of injuries that could not be cared for by the school nurse. Teachers were victimized as well as students by the gangs' indiscriminate violence. So mentally debilitating were their actions that whatever positive strides the school took on behalf of the majority of students who still wanted to learn were severely hampered by the fear and paranoia gangs generated. A student's worries no longer ended at being robbed of their lunch money or his locker being broken into. It had become a matter of survival, of life and death.

Still I believed the situation could be diffused. I was, somehow, in control. Then something happened that turned my life inside out.

Adam Parks was an A, B student with ambitions of becoming a civil rights attorney. He also spearheaded a student organization designed to combat the gang element at Salvation.

The organization worked. Students rallied around Adam to shove out the "thugs" and "hoodlums," to use Adam's words, and regain control of their school. Teachers and parents generously volunteered their time and energies to the cause. While the gangs maintained a visible presence wearing colors and the like, their strangling influence floundered considerably.

Dalton Stewart, an expelled gang leader I constantly attempted to keep away from school grounds, got into an argument with Adam in the schoolyard. This battle of words went back and forth until Dalton struck Adam in the face. Adam fought back. According to teachers who witnessed the incident from inside the school, gang members attempted to intercede but were thwarted by other students, mainly members of the wrestling and football teams. From what I saw of the two boys afterwards, Adam soundly whipped Dalton.

As much as I hated to, I had no choice but to exercise school policy. Adam I gave three days suspension. Dalton I had arrested for trespassing. Adam returned to school on November 11, 1984. He had stopped in my office prior to assembly to inform me of that fact and have the matter of his suspension closed. Adam was found in the fourth floor boys' bathroom on that day. He had been beaten with blunt instruments (in all likelihood baseball bats). He was unconscious. Numerous bones in his body were broken. Paul Jacobs, my then eleventh grade history teacher, found his contorted figure and came to me in tears. When I saw Adam, I fell to my knees. In all of my life, I had never experienced the depth of grief I felt at that moment. I shamelessly cried. I can recall someone leading me away by the arm. It was my hard-nosed secretary, Mrs. Olsen. She was crying too.

Adam Renaldo Parks miraculously lived but as a vegetable confined to a bed and a wheelchair. Students at Salvation organized a rally to be held at Schenley Park in his honor. The Board of Education, the Mayor, the Police Chief, students, teachers, and principals from all over the city attended. Storm clouds darkened the sky. Humidity dampened the skin. There were variegated speeches filled with well-intentioned promises. People wept, prayed, questioned, speculated, and seethed. I remember little of my own speech about Adam. It was said I spoke with a bold voice in proud terms of a young man I unabashedly claimed to love. I do remember my knees shaking, my heart pounding, warm tears mixing with the film of perspiration on my face. There were flowers in full bloom somewhere on the grounds. I overheard someone say, "It was beautiful as funerals go."

Those phantom words proved to be prophetic. Adam swiftly became a tragic memory filed in the back of our minds. I visited him every Wednesday at Children's hospital until his death. He became my fatal reminder of courage.

I've never married or fathered children of my own. I suppose you might say that I have adopted the children of Salvation as my family. As do parents in most families one tries to maintain balance, a sense of fairness for all its members. Equally true is the attachment one sometimes develops for certain members that does not extend to the others. The exceptionally bright ones, the children of promise, those are the persons that uncork a fondness in me I imagine I would direct toward my own son or daughter. Godfrey Booke is one such child. He is gifted in many ways that remind me of a rough-edged Adam Parks. That's why I ride him. I see it as my job to liberate children like him from here both alive and prepared for a future. The others . . . well, all I can say for them, if they need help, look for my hand. It will always be there.

I buried a large portion of my hopes alongside Adam. While I still believe in education and the children at Salvation, I wonder if I have the strength or understanding to do what it takes to salvage these young lives. Where did all the answers go?

STORY NINE

Fresh from the kill zone
-- The Prophet

The year was 1967. Don't remember what month, week, or day. We were on patrol in the DMZ. Discovered NVR occupation, met with two firefights and one ambush. It was raining, had been for the last seventeen wake-ups. Everything we had was waterlogged or rotted. We stank, we had little sleep, and most of our C-rations were spoiled. Cat-size rats were all over the place. All kinds of jungle creatures crawled inside our ponchos, fatigues, boots, helmets, anywhere they could fit, trying to keep dry and warm, a regular paradise.

After the ambush, we pulled back. As if we hadn't been through enough, LT force-marched our dead tired asses the last five miles back to Quang Tri, our home base.

Fresh from the kill zone, three wounded six dead. We survivors wondered if our number was next.

Aside from three hots and a cot, there was nothing else for line grunts to do at base, except clean themselves up and cool out, try to forget Charlie for a bit. Maybe you did for a minute . . . if you were lucky.

There was this dude in our unit we called Slick. Dude was a Boney Maroney type with a processed hairdo. The 'do is why we dubbed him Slick. He hailed from Louisiana, and every syllable out of his mouth tipped you to that fact.

I'd been in 'Nam a few months. Seen brothers like him come and go most of them in body bags; ready to kick gook ass for good old Uncle Sam, march home with a shit-eating grin on their face, waving Old Glory. Fresh grunt meat for the VC guerrillas, that's how I had him pegged.

My personal belief about the Vietnamese people was the same as Muhammad Ali. They hadn't done nothing to me. I had nothing against them. Leave 'em the fuck alone.

Then I was drafted. I decided not to resist. Better to do my time in the army, than in the pen -- or on the run.

How bad could the service be? Sgt. Chip Saunders always came out of it all right, smiling and shit, why not me? Was I really that naïve, or simply stupid?

Then I got to 'Nam and reality kicked in. Pissed and shit my pants during my first firefight. Bullets and asses were flying everywhere. It wasn't well-organized military maneuvers but on-the-spot survival tactics.

That word, survival, became the key principle behind all combat. Survival became my prime objective, my supreme instinct. It's an ugly word, not to be spoken with pride. It accepts no race or religion and doesn't recognize gender or age. Its face is scratched and grimy and scared, with rabid teeth greedily snapping at the glimmering silk threads of life. What frightened me most was that one day, I woke up, and that face belonged to me.

I got off track again. I'm always doing that. I'm going to have to work on my concentration if I'm going to continue to serve the Lord.

Day after we got back to camp, me, Jay, Taylor, Daryl, Jazz, and Wilson were in our barracks, kicked back on our cots, doing a lot of nothing when Slick came over talking shit about his wife.

He showed off some pictures of her. (I think her name was Flora). Told us proudly she was pregnant. Slick didn't need to say a thing. The way her belly was swollen looked like she swallowed a whole watermelon, rind and all.

We got on his case. Jay told Slick she wasn't pregnant just fat. Taylor asked him who the father was. Daryl let him know of his deepest fear the kid would turn out butt-ugly like him, and Jazz swore he knew her intimately. Wilson congratulated him on having such a lovely wife, and then asked if she'd been blind since birth. By the time I got my two cents in all the good ones had been copped. All that was left to say was it looked like him with a wig and a basketball stuffed under his blouse.

Slick was cool. For every one rip the fellows laid on him, he came back with at least two of his own. That guaranteed acceptance in our squad, especially after the expert way he handled himself during that last VC ambush we encountered while on patrol. Fit in like he'd been in the bush for years, instead of the raw grunt we assumed he was. And that was definitely righteous.

There was something else about Slick makes me smile even now thinking back. You know, the kind of person can make you laugh during the worst of times? That was Slick. He shot lifeblood back into the battle-weary bodies of our jaded unit. Refreshed our memories, forced us to think about the good things back home, things that can keep a man focused and purposeful in his duties. In short, he gave us back our will to do more than survive. He reintroduced us to living.

Got so we believed in Slick, he became our indestructible warrior. No matter what Charlie threw our way, Slick found a way for us to throw it back in triplicate.

But the bush does strange things to the sanest of men. Had my own trip that it was the training ground for Satan when he was designing Hell. Brother Wilson said it best: "Two things that'll surely get you killed in 'Nam: caring too much or too little." The latter happened to Slick.

Three days after we got out of the bush, we were right back in it. Our unit teamed up with K Platoon. Both squads were under the command of LT Frier, an LT with good field experience, known for carrying out missions with minimal casualties. That damn sure wasn't the case with the gung-ho motherfucker we previously served under.

Reports had been received that VC were operating in our area. Our job was to recon a ridgeline where the suspected VC had dug in.

Night before we left there was a break in the rain. Ground was still soft. Bush was denser than week-old split pea soup. LT forced us to stick to the trail (even though it would have taken half the time through the jungle). But any attempt to hack our way through would only warn Charlie of our approach, perfect setup for a VC ambush.

There was not one confrontation during the whole twenty-mile hump. That was usually a good sign. Meant VC were concentrated somewhere else.

We arrived at the ridge at about 1500 hours. Things were quiet. Jungle looked deserted.

Slick was our "Kit Carson" scout. He went in to verify a VC presence and their position. At LT's command, we cooled our heels and waited for Slick to return.

1630. Slick came back and reported seeing seven bamboo structures that resembled crude bunkers along the eastern flank of the ridge about two klicks ahead. He determined there were fourteen VC, tops, with no more than AK-47's in their arsenal. There were no signs of booby traps or other enemy troops.

LT ordered us to "lock and load." Then he ordered me to position myself along the south rim of the ridge, keeping an eye out for any possible backdoor assaults or attempted VC escapes. The rest of the grunts moved in.

I nested myself on a bluff looking down into the small VC encampment and watched it go down.

Things looked smooth for a while. The LT had the men moving in low and slow. I got my sights on the third bunker from the left. Had a straight line down into it, kept one eye on the grunts.

Gunfire broke out from the bunker farthest from me. Guess one of the VC heard something.

Shit didn't last but a minute. What wasn't riddled with bullets got blown to hell by frags. They didn't even have time for P & P -- prayers and promises. We didn't lose a man, a real American success story.

Slick was right, there were only fourteen. Five of the dead were women, one a boy no older than twelve, the rest, Vietnamese men. We moved around checking out the bodies, looking inside the bunkers, our nerves still edgy, expecting something more to happen.

I never got used to killing only its necessity.

That was Slick's first encounter with VC in the persons of a child and women. You can't be sure who you take out during a battle. Just keep firing until the firing stops. Bunkers make it all the worse. Mostly all you see are heads and rifles popping up and down. How the fuck you going tell who you're firing at? Even if you could, would it matter? I'm sure Slick knew that, probably questioned if he was the one who did it. Knowing Slick, he'd say something like, "It shouldn't have gone down like that. Don't matter, VC, whoever, should've went down another way."

Anyway, LT ordered the area secured. Slick and I were buddied up, ready to move out, when I caught him looking down at the blown-out back of the head of one of the VC; kept staring at it like it was his mother.

He kicked it over. It made the death sigh. Body was fucked, what was left of it. Bullet had punched out a clean hole in the right side of her forehead. Her eyes were open, glassy, shock lacquered over them. She reminded me of Camille. I turned my head.

Slick couldn't stop staring at her. I tried to pull him away but he shoved me back. I forced myself to look at her again, a girl, about fifteen, well pregnant. That was all I could stand. I had to walk away. Left Slick standing there staring.

I told the platoon sergeant about him. Sarge finally got Slick to move.

We secured the area. We patrolled the perimeter bush for two days. We didn't find anything. Not even a whiff of Charlie. Then the rain came back.

Slick had gotten lockjaw. He didn't say anything to nobody about nothing. He functioned okay. Did his job, obeyed orders, no sweat. But not one word did the brother whisper in all that time. He didn't rip back if somebody said something about him or his family. Wouldn't even say yes sir to orders, just give up a deaf nod and go do whatever he was ordered to do.

A few of the dudes from K Platoon took to calling him Zombie. Caused more than a few fistfights when one of them said it around the wrong brother, especially when they tried saying he was working on a Section B. We knew Slick better than that.

On the fourth day, through the rain, we pulled back to base, no problems, no incidents. Slick still wasn't talking.

When we got to base, mail from the States was waiting for us. Slick had a couple of letters. He just pocketed them and went off somewhere.

Everybody read their mail, passed around pictures, and shared goodies from home that managed to make it through, shit like that. In the middle of the whole thing it dawned on me, I hadn't seen Slick for a while. I went looking for him, couldn't find him nowhere. Kept it to myself and slipped back into the groove of the festivities with no one apparently having missed me.

Next day, word was out. Slick went AWOL. The Brothers didn't believe it but nobody knew where he was.

A couple of days go by, no Slick. Taylor and me rifled through his gear before the MPs came to claim it. We were hoping to find a clue where Slick might be, so we could bring him back and make up some cock-and-bull story about where he'd been.

We found a crumpled letter from his father stuffed in his duffel bag. When we opened it, first thing fell out was his dog tags, dried blood on the chain.

There had been an accident. His father was bringing Flora and his newborn son home from the hospital when they met with the Klan. They forced his father off the road and harassed them. In trying to protect the baby, Flora got hit in the head with a club. She fell. The baby slipped out of her arms. His son died before they could get him to a hospital that would accept coloreds.

The Brothers and me never found Slick. Far as we know, neither did the Army. Wished you would've talked to us, given us a chance. Maybe we could have injected into you some of that spirit you laid on us when we needed it most. I owe you my life, Slick. It's damn little right now but that's okay. Wherever you are good brother, I miss you.

STORY TEN

The simpler the soul, the clearer the vision
-- Josephine Louise Johnson

A woman in her sixties, hair of silvery gray, bronze skin deepened to a reddish brown by constant exposure to the sun. A somewhat weathered, drooping face. Her large dark brown eyes had required the assistance of eyeglasses to read since the age of forty-one. Her plump body was filled with the annoying aches, pains, and stiffness of her years. A grandmother, a great-grandmother, she did not exercise to prevent age from having its way. She only altered her meals according to her culinary taste and digestive disposition. The lady in question had not been a career woman. She had never desired to be more than a good mother and wife. Those things she believed she had achieved.

Josephine Johnson rooted through the attic in search of a clear crystal vase to place her colorful bouquet of fresh cut flowers. She had harvested the flowers from her modest backyard garden. The vase she had in mind would be the perfect centerpiece, in combination with the flowers, for her dining room table. She knew it was there. Exactly where was the challenge.

The attic had been stuffy when she arrived. Josephine had opened the windows to air it out. The heat and humidity seemed only to make matters worse. It did not trouble the veteran of decades of hot, humid Pittsburgh summers, dressed in a powder blue sleeveless blouse and blue jeans. From experience, Josephine knew enough to keep a small jug of ice water and a cotton hand towel nearby to wipe away perspiration.

Josephine had been searching for close to two hours and was only a quarter of the way through the stacks of unlabeled cardboard boxes. Organized clutter is what she called their attic. Things were stacked, piled, or positioned with nothing more in mind than to find an out-of-the-way place for them. There was no one person to blame. Carl, herself, and at one time, Gratey, had contributed to the stockpile. One she vowed to deplete before another summer came and went.

During her search, Josephine had encountered numerous memorabilia. Items she thought lost or gone forever had found residence in obscurity. She thwarted temptations to linger over objects that threatened nostalgia by remaining focused on her goal. Her persistence paid off.

In the same box next to the crystal vase, Josephine found a pleasant surprise. A hand-made porcelain cookie jar decorated with hand-painted roses, ribbons, and bells. It had been a wedding gift from her grandmother. In memory of the little girl who raided her cookie jar every chance she had. When, why, or how it made it into the attic she could not recall.

The cookie jar accompanied Josephine downstairs along with the vase. She left behind the mess she had made in the attic. Carl would take care of it. All she had to do was mention it to him and he would restore it to its manageable state. After all Josephine had been through to find the vase, the very least Carl could do was put everything back as it was. Josephine smiled to herself. *It would give him something to gripe about*, she thought. *Get him out of that recliner and away from that television for a few of hours.*

Steam rose from the soapy hot water in the kitchen sink. Josephine immersed the vase and the lid of the cookie jar in the water. She was about to place the cookie jar into its sudsy depths when she noticed something inside. Josephine spread out a couple of paper towels onto the kitchen table, emptying the jar's contents onto them. A rectangular package wrapped in cheesecloth and loosely bound by white thread tumbled out. Josephine placed the cookie jar in the water, and then thoroughly dried her hands. She would let the vase, cookie jar, and lid soak for a while. That would make the greasy grit that formed on their surfaces due to so many years of oppressive storage a lot easier to wash away.

Josephine had left the television on in the living room. Its constant chatter kept her company when Carl was not home. She had wiped the dust from the package with a dry dishcloth. Josephine made herself comfortable in Carl's recliner, and then unwrapped the package. The photographs brought it all back.

It was a school day. A little more than a year after Camille had died. The heavens cried for her. Josephine was next door visiting with her best friend Lorraine. She returned home to find Carl indiscriminately burning photographs in the fireplace. Carl had struggled mightily with the loss of their daughter, as had Josephine. Somehow, Carl had come to the unwarranted conclusion that destroying photographs was what he needed to do to release himself from the constant woe of his daughter's death. It was his way of incinerating his past in an effort to find peace in his future. By the time Josephine discovered Carl doing this, his mind was fervently fixed on his purpose. Josephine could not stop him. When she tried, Carl forcefully shoved her away.

Josephine did what she could. Fortunately, they kept their photographs in various places around the house, in shoeboxes, small brown paper bags, and scattered throughout junk drawers. Josephine gathered up every photograph she could find and rushed out of the back door to her neighbor's house.

Lorraine's husband, Marcus, and Carl were good friends. Marcus managed to settle Carl down. Josephine kept the salvaged photographs at her neighbors with their blessings. She was concerned Carl might have a relapse and attempt to destroy them as well.

Even after Carl stabilized, Josephine was not taking any chances. She took the photographs she had rescued from the flames and wrapped them in cheesecloth, in an effort to protect them from the elements without damaging the prints, and hid them inside the cookie jar she had not used for years. To make certain nothing would happen to them, Josephine packed the cookie jar in a box with her crystal vase and a few other items to be stored in the attic. Carl delivered the box to the attic never knowing the pictures were inside. Josephine had expected to retrieve them later. A time capsule if you will. One she fully intended to revisit with her husband once the pain of Camille's passing had lessened to a bearable degree. That day did not come soon enough. Selective amnesia got there first. The small stack of black-and-white photographs she held in her hands were all that survived that tragic ordeal.

Josephine fingered the top photograph. It was a picture of Gratey. He could not have been more than one month old. It brought back a flood of warm memories. Gratey was a handsome child with a full head of curly black hair, cute smile and bright eyes. Worth the eighteen hours of labor Josephine endured to bring him into this world, all eight pounds, two ounces of him. But then Josephine supposed every mother believed her child was precious, adorable, handsome, or beautiful. She was no different, she was proud to say.

Gratey was an easy-going infant. He liked to laugh, play, and wrestle with his father. They were optimistic for his future. His sister's death, and Vietnam, culminated to send him into a depressive tailspin Josephine had begun to believe he would never pull out of alive. Now it was enough he was no longer addicted to drugs or alcohol. Josephine knew of his unorthodox preaching and strange appearance. He explained to his mother that it was all a part of his plan to awaken people to biblical teachings and move them from the sinful toward the sanctified. Josephine told him she mostly wished he would cut his hair, shave, and wear some decent clothes for himself and God. It would not hurt for him to visit his parents every once in a while, she added. Gratey apologized promising that he would. A promise he had not kept as of yet.

Staring at the photograph, her grandmother came to mind. "The simpler the soul, the clearer the vision," her grandmother always said about babies. Her grandmother believed children came into this world knowing their destiny. It was only after adults polluted their trust of their "inner eyes," as she put it, did they lose sight. Josephine wondered if at some time her own son knew how his life would unfold. If he did, could he have changed things? Can anyone alter the templates of fate?

The next photograph was a picture of Gratey and herself. Gratey was around eighteen months old. He was standing, holding onto his mother's long pleated skirt, smiling as usual, a couple of teeth to show for his effort. Gratey was walking by then and was prone to get into everything. He was always taking on some new adventure with a cackling laugh or a devilish gleam in his eyes. Carl had taken the picture during an impromptu picnic they had at Schenley Park. It was a summer Thursday afternoon. Not a holiday so the park was not crowded. The day had been muggy, but the rain stayed away. Josephine wanted to bask in her amiable memory for a soothing moment. She stared at the photograph for a while allowing the picnic to replay in her mind.

Each photograph accentuated some fond recollection of her life. She felt blessed they covered such a diverse cross-section of familiar souls. Photographs of Carl, herself, Gratey, uncles, aunts, cousins, nieces, nephews, friends, a couple of wedding pictures, and one Josephine was ill prepared to see.

Her memory of that day was as vivid as if it were happening before her. Camille was sitting on Gratey's lap. Gratey was smiling. Camille was laughing. Carl had taken the photograph, posing the children as he had seen done in professional shots. They had not planned to have children so far apart. It simply worked out that way. She and Carl believed it worked out for the best. Her children loved each other. The photograph proved that without question.

Josephine was not ready for the deep agony that erupted in her heart. She had truly believed she had found closure over the years regarding Camille. Seeing the photograph only proved she was wrong. In truth, there was still something left of her grief. A brutal anguish buried deeper in her person than she realized. Josephine would have forfeited her life, her soul, to make that photograph she held flesh. It was not to be, not now, not ever. In some dimly lit place of foolish expectation, a drop of denial still lingered. That was where Josephine secretly clung to an irrational belief, that by some divine miracle, Camille would arise.

Her hands trembled as she held fast to the photograph of her daughter and her son. Josephine refused to look away. Refused to disavow the torment she had obviously suppressed for so long. Carl had his moment of closure when he attempted to incinerate their past. Now was her time to experience her catharsis. Camille was dead. Josephine loved her and wished it were not so, but her daughter was gone forever. An excruciating truth she had to accept, if not for herself, then for her daughter. Josephine was certain Camille would have wanted it that way. Josephine's tears stained the black-and-white still life, falling freely and without shame.

STORY ELEVEN

Forgiveness is not earned. It is the ultimate sacrifice
-- Tehra Deniece Thompson

"Anthony stop that! You know better than to beat on that coffee table with your toy hammer, making all that racket. That table's already got enough nicks on it as it is."

That boy, that boy, that boy, all morning he has terrorized the house, beating just about everything he could with that toy hammer of his. He's in his terrible two's and getting on my last nerve.

"Don't give me that look like you don't know what I'm talking about. You know what I'm saying." Anthony smiles at me. Usually his cute dimples make me melt. I raised my eyebrows to show him I meant business. He raised his hammer over his head, grinning by then. What could I do? I adore my son. He may only be two but he knows he's my weakness. That threat of disobedience would normally be my cue to chase him around the room, hug him, play with, kiss and tickle him. Become a part of his game. But I'm seven months pregnant with my second child. Today, I'm just too tired, too bloated, and in need of a break. This heat isn't helping at all. I called my mother earlier, hoping she would be able to take her only grandchild off my hands for a while. She wasn't home. I'll try again later.

"Come here Anthony," I tell him. My son stops grinning. I only want to check his shorts to see if he's gone to the bathroom in them. I repeat my command. He makes his way to me, doubtful, hesitant, uncertain of my intentions, dropping his hammer on the floor before he takes his first step. Smart child, too smart sometimes, he knows his mama. I'd take that hammer from him and hide it. His plan was to make my taking possession of his nerve-wracking toy as challenging as possible.

When Anthony got close enough, I firmly, but gently, pulled him to me. He didn't resist. I check his pants while he talks to me in a language only other two-year-olds understand. There was nothing in his pants but the sweet fragrance of baby powder. After I hugged and kissed him, I struggled to my feet. Anthony tried to help by tugging on my smock. He made me laugh. He laughed too. I picked him up and took him into his room, wading through his toys, which were everywhere. I'll have him pick them up later. Right now, it's naptime for this little guy and rest period for me. Anthony doesn't resist. That tells me how tired he is. A couple of minutes after I laid him down in his bed, he was fast asleep.

I made my way from Anthony's bedroom to the kitchen, forcing myself to ignore his toys and the rest of the mess my living room was in. A cozy cup of chamomile tea and some vanilla wafers will hit the spot. Wish Herman were here to get them for me. Need to call my husband at work to make sure he remembers to bring home more milk and diapers. Oh well, guess I'll just stand by the stove until this water's ready, won't take but a minute. If I sit down now it'll be tough getting up.

I must be crazy craving a hot drink on a hot day like today. Must be the baby's doing. No reason I can't rustle up those vanilla wafers while I wait for the water to boil. A little lime sherbet would go good with those wafers. Two scoops. Don't want to overdo it. Water's ready and so am I. Let me sit down here at this kitchen table and enjoy my snack. Good Lord, feels good to take a load off. My back is killing me. Before I eat anything, let me say grace. "Dear Lord, bless this food I'm about to eat. And bless all those who love me and I them. Amen; time to feast."

I'm worried about my family. Not my family as in Herman or Anthony or our blessing on its way, our faith is strong. We are well cared for by our creator and savior, Jesus Christ. My brothers and mom cause me concern. None of them fully accepts Jesus Christ as their savior. They have yet to realize, without him to guide their lives, they cannot enter the Kingdom of Heaven. Aside from their souls, how can they ever expect to live full, righteous lives without embracing the true son of God?

Take Godfrey, for instance. My little brother is the smartest -- and dumbest -- person I know. Every chance he gets he starts trouble for himself. He's stealing and lying and fornicating and cursing and blaspheming and God knows what other sins he's guilty of. Mom pretends she doesn't know he steals. Hopefully Godfrey will stop before it's too late and he gets caught. If nothing else, he should have learned something from his older brother, Nat. Like it says in the scripture, Book of Proverbs "The wise man is glad to be instructed, but a self-sufficient fool falls flat on his face."

I am concerned for Godfrey's soul. Sometimes I fear his soul may be so influenced by the dark specter of Satan, he may be beyond redemption, beyond salvation. Every time Herman and I try talking to Godfrey about straightening out his life, all he does is ridicule our beliefs and us. If there's anything Godfrey understands it's irreverence. He lectures us in his smart-aleck way about his philosophies on God and the universe. He stresses that what we believe, or know to be true, is archaic and delusive. My little brother speaks to us in the same fashion he used to do when we were children that caused me to cold conk him.

Mom says I should love and support and pray for him regardless. I do all of these things when Godfrey allows me. I pray for him even when he doesn't. "Forgiveness is not earned. It is the ultimate sacrifice." That's what the pastor said in one of his Sunday services. "Forgiveness is absolute. Forgiveness is instant, or it is not forgiveness."

While I agree with those words there are certain things I will not tolerate under my roof or in any house of the Lord. Blaspheming is one of them, and Godfrey knows it. He can make me so mad sometimes it takes all of my strength not to wash my hands of him. God continues to answer my prayers for wisdom and courage and patience. One day Godfrey will see the light and its name will be Jesus Christ, amen. Like the good book says: "Anyone willing to be corrected is on the pathway to life. Anyone refusing has lost his chance." I will not allow my baby brother to forfeit his opportunity at everlasting life. Even if I have to cold conk him to make him see the truth.

Nat is my older brother, the oldest of three children. It breaks my heart to see him dealing drugs. Growing up, Nat and I were very close. He was in every sense my older brother. Protector, advisor, tutor, and for a while my most trusted confidant. That was until I told Nat about the first time I had sex. That was before I found Jesus Christ, or, before Jesus Christ found me. Back before I accepted that it was a sin to fornicate.

It was with Tevin Marshall, an awful experience. Neither of us knew what we were doing. I was more glad when it was over than anything.

The first of my family to discover I was no longer a virgin was my mother. I didn't volunteer the information. She noticed something was wrong with me as soon as I walked in the door. At first, she thought I might be coming down with something. Mom checked my temperature, felt my adenoids, and looked down my throat, searching for signs of an impending cold, flu or fever.

During my mother's examination of me, something must have clicked. A woman can look at another woman and tell a lot about her from what she sees. If the woman you are scrutinizing happens to be your daughter, that insight is magnified a hundred fold. Mom took me into her bedroom where we had a private talk. When she finally got it out of me, my mother was not pleased. Nonetheless, she helped me through it with a hot water bottle, hot tea with honey, lemon, and a little brandy, and lots of parental advice.

Godfrey figured out what had happened by the way mom and I were behaving. Like I said, Godfrey's as smart as they come. Nat had been at football practice and didn't get home until late that evening. Nobody told him anything. The next evening, Nat was tutoring me in math when he mentioned a rumor he had heard at school that Tevin and I had been, as Nat put it, intimate. I was concentrating so hard on the math problem I was working on I simply responded. I told Nat it was true. Nat finished helping me, kissed me on the forehead, told me he loved me and congratulated me on how well I was doing in my studies and left. I assumed he was going to hang out with his football buddies. Something he did a lot of back then.

The next day, I heard Tevin was in the hospital. Nat had beaten him up for violating me. I also heard through the high school grapevine that Nat told Tevin if he ever came near me again his next stop would be the mortuary. When I confronted Nat with all of those charges, he confessed. I was so furious with Nat I didn't speak to him for four days. I went to visit Tevin in the hospital but they wouldn't let me in because I wasn't family. Fortunately for Nat, Tevin never pressed charges. Since there were no witnesses, it was Tevin's word against my brother's. Nat's word carried more clout because of his high school football prowess. Not to mention, I think Tevin was afraid of what the football team would do to him if he decided to press charges against my big brother.

I finally started speaking to Nat again because he looked so miserable about the whole thing. He wasn't dejected because he beat up Tevin but because he never meant to hurt his little sister.

Nat and I discussed his actions. He told me it was for my own good. As the man of the family, he felt, it was his responsibility to protect us. By that, he meant my mom and me. That blanket of protection didn't include Godfrey because Godfrey wasn't having it. The only person Godfrey ever listened to was mom. That hasn't changed.

Anyway, I told Nat I didn't understand where he was coming from. Why was it all right for him to have sex without being married and I couldn't? What made matters worse was mom agreed with Nat. An unwanted pregnancy was the biggest reason they kept bringing up as well as the possibility of contacting sexually transmitted diseases. Respect for oneself was another key point. Apparently, self-respecting women didn't have sex. They merely fantasized about it. One should strive to remain virtuous for the man she would marry. Blinded by hormones and stubbornness, I told Nat and mom they were being ridiculous. I informed them that these days, women were doing things differently. Women were making their own rules. While I don't remember all of it, it was a good speech from an intellectual standpoint. Little did they realize my experience with Tevin had been such a turnoff, I had no intention of fornicating any time soon.

Nat and mom were right, however. I should have waited until I was married. I know that now, although their arguments against fornication were strictly social and medical, not biblical.

It was a crime, not God that forever changed my relationship with my big brother. Nat had a friend. David Carlson. They were close. Even though they were the same age, Nat treated David like a little brother. I suppose to Nat, David was more of the little brother he envisioned Godfrey should have been. David allowed Nat to help him. Godfrey rebelled at Nat's every attempt. Why, who knows with Godfrey? As far as I can remember, Godfrey was always that way. Even as a baby. Anyone but mom would try to change him or feed him or play with him and he would scream his head off. My baby brother is a strange child that only God can save now.

David got a girl by the name of Carrie Washington pregnant. David was very much in love with Carrie. Everybody at Salvation knew that. So nobody was surprised when David tried to do the right thing by her. Except Carrie had gotten an abortion before she told David. David still wanted to marry her.

Like most young couples, money was a problem. Nat wanted to help. Nat got the idea to rob a grocery store. Somebody told him it was easy money. David and Nat were caught, tried, and convicted.

Prison changes a person. A person you love, someone you've spent your whole life with and you think you know becomes a complete stranger. Not overnight, but gradually. I watched it happen to Nat. I made it a point to visit him once a week, as did mom -- and surprisingly, so did Godfrey. That's one thing I will say about Godfrey, when things are at their worst, he's the first in line to help. As soon as things get better he's gone. He's odd like that. Most people are the opposite.

The first couple of months Nat was in prison, he was his usual self, upbeat, brash, and somewhat cocky. Little by little, he became more introverted. His expressions hardened like somebody had poured concrete into his veins. His eyes began to look crazed. For the first time in my life, I was actually frightened of my big brother. But I never stopped visiting or supporting him. Neither did the rest of our family.

I missed Nat. I missed his strong male presence in my life. Mom was there. She did everything she could. My dad was in no condition to be a father. He needed help himself. The type of help none of us could provide.

It was after one of my Saturday visits with Nat that I happened by Ezekiel Baptist Church. It was a beautiful day full of warm sunlight and gentle breezes. My soul was heavy with the burden of Nat's incarceration. Nothing I did ever seemed to lift that weight from my heart. The choir was singing "Oh Happy Day." Their voices rolled out of that church like thunder over a clear horizon. It was God's work, I know now, bringing me home. Then it was only the beginning of a series of revelations that put me on the path to righteousness.

I stepped inside. The church was nearly full. I found myself sitting, kind of hunched down, all the way back in the farthest pew. I don't remember taking the steps to get there. Until this day, I believe the Lord reached down, plucked me up, and sat me down inside that church. His way of introducing himself to this lost soul wandering the wasteland of sin.

The choir sounded even better inside. Their voices resounded throughout the church. They sang, "Precious Lord" followed by "Nearer, My God to Thee." I found myself swaying to the music, wanting to sing along. By the time the pastor stepped up to the pulpit, I was ready to listen.

He spoke of the trials of Job. How God allowed Satan to have his way with one of his most devoted servants, only to have Job prove his unswerving faith in his Creator. At the end of his sermon, the pastor asked all of those who were prepared to accept Jesus Christ as their savior to step forward and be baptized in the name of the Lord. I got in line. It was a long line. When I was about halfway there, I got scared. Satan sprinkled ashes of doubt on my mind. I left, planning to give what the pastor said more thought.

Two days later, I ran into a group of teenagers at our school who called themselves God's People -- or G.P. for short. "Bible thumpers" is how they were known around Salvation. As many times as I had seen those teenagers around the school, never before had they approached me. On that day, they invited me to go with them to a prayer meeting after school. I went. I listened. I liked what I heard. More so, I liked what they believed so I joined.

The following Sunday, I returned to Ezekiel Baptist where I was baptized in the name of our Lord, our savior, Jesus Christ, amen. Believe it or not, I was afraid Nat wouldn't approve of my becoming a Bible thumper. I didn't mention my acceptance of Jesus Christ into my life until Nat was released from prison. I asked the rest of the family to remain mute on the topic as well. It turned out, Nat found out from friends on the outside. During the entire time of his incarceration he never let on that he knew. It was at my wedding Nat told me he was pleased I found something that gave me so much peace. He hoped to one day find something that would do the same for him. Ironically, it was Nat who started me down the righteous path of salvation. I owe him nothing less than to help him discover his own path to redemption.

For the past two Sundays, Nat has gone to church with us. He still hasn't accepted Jesus Christ into his life, but he has agreed to continue accompanying us to Sunday services.

Good Lord, that boy's kicking me again. I know it's a boy. Don't need any kind of test to tell me that. He feels just like Anthony did in the womb except this one kicks like a mule. I'll have another sip of this chamomile tea. That'll help settle you down a little. There now, that's better.

Now my mother is a different story. Besides worrying about my brothers -- her sons -- she's doing just fine . . . mostly. Her biggest pitfall is her heart. Family brings the most joy into your life and the most pain. She still pines for my father. After all of these years, after all of the grief he's caused her, she still loves him. If you ask her, she'll proudly tell you so. I pray that mom will soon find the strength to let my father go. Accept the inevitable. Then she could get on with her life. Marry Chris Devlin. That man loves her with all his being, as much as life itself. Chris is a reliable man. He'll take good care of her. Only her children and God could possibly love her more.

I'll admit Chris's not as righteous as I would like. Neither him nor my mother walk in the full light of Jesus Christ. I suppose some could say the same about me. They do what they can. I see them together in church just about every Sunday. Although it is my opinion, they've had one too many Saturday nights at those smoky jazz clubs, traipsing and drinking with the devil. I won't go into what else they've been doing of which the Lord would not approve. Mom says she's a grown woman with good common sense who can pretty much do what she wants. I say she's grown enough to know better. Not out loud of course. Just in my mind. I respect her too much to do otherwise. She is -- and will always be no matter what -- my one and only mother.

I only pray mom marries Chris. Together they could find the holy path to redemption. I know, one day, they will accept Jesus Christ as their Savior, if they would simply open their hearts to the Lord as they have each other. Then they could know eternal joy and eternal peace. The Bible says, "Hope deferred makes the heart sick; but when dreams come true at last, there is life and joy." Amen. If the good Lord wills it, so shall it be.

When it comes to my father, there is good reason for concern. At least he believes in God, which is more than I can say for that heathen baby brother of mine. I saw my father near Kaufmann's the other day. Godfrey had told me about him. I wanted a firsthand look to see how he was. He was preaching, yelling at people to change their sinful lives, just plain acting crazy. From a distance, I listened to what he had to say for a few minutes. I will say this much for my dad. He knows his scriptures. From what little I heard, his biblical quotes were right on.

When I got near him, he almost hit me with his walking stick. He didn't mean to. I happened to walk up to him during a part of his sermon when he abruptly raised his arms to the sky. His stick whipped right over my head in a blind arc. I had no chance to get out of the way especially in my condition. I suppose he didn't expect anyone to be that close to him with the way he was behaving. Most people took a wide berth around my father.

I remember my father as he was when I was a very young child. He was a volatile man. Prone to say or do anything at a moment's notice. Though his physical rage was vented only at inanimate objects, his verbal abuses were vicious. Words can strike blows much deeper than any dealt by the hand. My father at times reached those places in all of us, most especially my mother. Through it all, my mother never had a bad word to say about my father.

We never could figure out why he hated us so much. It got to the point we avoided our father as much as possible. When he left, for Nat and me -- Godfrey was only a baby then -- it was welcome news.

After my father left us, our lives settled down. I found it strange that with all of his faults, I missed him. I guess I felt it was better to have an abusive father than no father at all.

When our father would return from his hiatus, Nat and I would visit him once a week, initially at mom's insistence. We always went together. Dad would have a gift for each of us along with a few dollars. I still wear the gold crucifix he gave me. So does Nat. I wonder what a psychiatrist would make of that.

At first, we were apprehensive. The man we knew was one to be feared. This new reserved attitude, softened demeanor, and calm voice were to be viewed with caution. Every child wants to love its parents. I guess that's why it shouldn't have surprised me when he won us over.

For a while, there was a lot we had to say to each other. He told us about his internal demons, his bouts with alcohol and drugs. The nightmare called Vietnam and his never-ending anguish over Camille. He told us of how much he loved and respected our mother and the reasons he had to leave. There was hope we would be reunited for a time, only this time as a stable family. Along the way something in him snapped. Something only my father could explain. A mysterious internal demon he still wrestled with forced us away.

Progressively, Nat and I did more and more of the talking. It got to the point where dad hardly said more than two sentences. The rage had died away but our father far too often was depressed and distant. Nat and I found ourselves visiting him out of pity, not love. Children should not have to pity their parents. It's unnatural and unhealthy.

Out of the blue, our father forbid us to see him. That familiar rage returned to tell us in undeniable terms we weren't wanted in his life. For a long time I struggled with that. His unexplained expulsion of us made me angry. It was one thing to leave us. Our hatred of his abusive behavior carried us through his absence. Now that we loved him, accepted, and to some degree understood his pain, he dismissed us from his life the way God banished Adam and Eve from the Garden of Eden. We did as he demanded and stayed away. Not out of respect for his wishes but out of the bitterness we felt toward him for his emotional betrayal.

Nat was the one who told me our father had moved and left no forwarding address. Nat had intended on telling our dad off. Again, I felt a sense of loss, even a twitch of responsibility for his leaving. What could we possibly have done to merit such treatment? There is a lesson to be learned from every trial and tribulation. My father taught me something my mother already knew: a lesson in unconditional love. No matter what, he is my father and I will always love him. Forgiveness, just like the pastor said. Acceptance is the next step up that ladder of love.

Anyway, the other day, after my father almost clocked me, he looked down on me with fury in his eyes. He was mad enough to give me a piece of his mind --however much he might have left. He didn't speak. His mouth formed the words, "Good Lord." His eyes eclipsed from anger to surprise to fondness in one full sweep. My father recognized me all right. When he offered to help me walk across the street, I accepted. He gave me his arm. A strong arm, a mighty arm, I must admit. Like a doting father he helped me, making certain with a contemptuous glare or raising of his stick, no one bumped into me. While we crossed the street I talked, he listened. It took a minute for me to make it. My feet were swollen, my legs ached, and my back was sore, so I was taking my time. I didn't call him dad or father. He had a bashful smile the entire time.

Once we were on the other side of the street, my father asked if I were OK. I told him yes. He asked if I needed anything. I told him I was fine, thanking him for the escort. I handed him a piece of paper with my address and telephone number on it which was my purpose for being there. Then I invited him to dinner. There was a lump in his throat. Tears were in his eyes. When he touched my face, it reminded me of one of those cherished moments when I was a little girl and I was his beautiful princess and he my noble king. My father said he would try to make it before he returned to his street corner pulpit. I know he will do his best.

It makes me sad to see my dad in the state he's in. But the Lord works in mysterious ways. Maybe that's God's way of exorcising my father's demons and bringing him home to Jesus Christ.

Oh Lord, that boy's up all ready. Seems like only a minute ago I put him down. "Hold on sweetheart! Mommy's coming!" With lungs like Anthony's, that child's destined to be a singer making sweet music for the Lord. I only ask the good Lord to have my son save a little of that music until he's old enough to know what to do with it. For now, please give my ears a break. I can't believe I ate that whole box of vanilla wafers and I'm still hungry.

STORY TWELVE

Only shadows and dust
-- Carlton Winslow Johnson

Gratey had been away at Army boot camp for a month when I wandered into his room. It was neat, organized, not the way Gratey kept it when he lived here. There were no smelly sneakers, clothes strewn about, games and 45's to be put away, or open books littering an unmade bed. It was tidy, the way my Josephine keeps things. Admittedly, I did not see Josephine clean his room, but I am certain she was why it appeared livable.

I missed Gratey though I didn't show it much. Josephine had gone grocery shopping, and I gave myself the excuse that his room needed airing out as a reason to enter. I opened the door and walked in. We had kept the door closed since Gratey left. The curtains were open, which allowed the sun to parade its irregular shapes along the edges of the brown carpet. The first thing I was going to do was open both windows and usher in those fresh spring breezes I had enjoyed on the walk home from work. As I reached down to pull open the northeast window, I heard something. It sounded like it came from the bed. When I turned and looked, there was nothing there. After I opened the window, I checked under the bed, only shadows and dust. As I was about to leave I heard it again. It sounded like a child giggling, except this time it seemed to come from the clothes closet. When I opened the door, there was nothing more than Gratey's clothes and shoes and a few cardboard boxes resting on the top shelf. No uninvited guests as I suspected.

Then I heard it once more, coming from behind me. Turning my head quickly I found myself staring straight out of the north window. I walked over and looked down upon the street. Two children were playing. I watched for a few minutes. A boy of about twelve and a girl of about six were playing It-tag. The boy, who was far more agile than his playmate, would tease the little girl by juking and back-pedaling faster than she could make adjustments to catch him. He laughed at her frustration. When she became angry and threatened to quit, he'd allow her to tag him only to pretend not to be able to catch her. This lasted a few sparse minutes, before he tagged the child and his teasing began anew. His laughter was what I had heard hiding about the room. He sounded precisely like Gratey when he was that young man's age.

Again, I attempted to leave when I realized something. Rarely had I spent time in Gratey's room. I would come in and wake him. Play games with him. Wrestle him. But never had I taken time to look around.

My eyes followed a sharp finger of sunlight along the carpet to the foot of his dresser. I wondered what was in those drawers. I walked over and opened them one at a time. Socks, underwear, T-shirts, pajamas, sweaters, play shirts, shorts, and a few small toys. Each drawer was accompanied by stale whiffs of clean clothes pent up too long. In the bottom right-hand drawer, shoved back in the far right corner, partially hidden under a small pile of briefs, was something that looked like a notebook. I reached in and pulled it out. The word "DIARY" was printed in gold inlaid letters on a black face cover. I backed up to the bed and sat down as I opened it, ignoring the guilt tugging at my conscience.

June 16, 1964

Our seventh grade English teacher, Mrs. Bourgeault, gave us an assignment. Actually, she gave us the option of whether or not to do it. She asked us to keep a summer diary. If we do, Mrs. Bourgeault promised we would receive no less than a C for the entire first semester of eighth grade. To make sure we did it during the summer, she is making us hand them in on the first day of school, so she can preview them. The girls in our class think it's a great idea. What do they know? I think it's stupid. I hate to write.

June 23, 1964

I don't know what to write about. Summer is fun. The days are hot, long, and sunny. I like that because it gives me a chance to play a lot. Mostly I play football, baseball and basketball at Miller Park. Miller Park is big, green, and friendly because a lot of my friends hang out there. I'm told that's what teenagers do. I wouldn't know. I'm only twelve. I haven't been a teenager long enough to know what's normal.

June 30, 1964

Marshall is my best friend. We first met in swim class in second grade. He is a forehead shorter than me. We look a lot alike. Both of us have "angular builds" and "crevada haircuts with a razor part on the side." (My dad described us that way. That is why I put them in quotes.) Marshall does not smile very much but he talks a lot. The dumbest thing I ever saw him do -- besides telling our fourth grade history teacher to go to hell, (I'm not sure if "go to hell" should be in quotes?). Anyway, the most impressive thing I ever saw him do was stand up to massive Conroy Fenning.

Conroy was a grade school bully who did not ask for things he took them. I got to the schoolyard just as Marshall was screaming up in Conroy's face "I ain't givin' you nothin'!" I was shocked. So was everybody else in the schoolyard. Then to top it off Marshall walked away grinning. Conroy did not do a thing. A few days later I found out Conroy was seeing Marshall's older sister, Mona.

For the last four years, I've tutored Marshall in math, history, English, and science. He has learned from me everything he knows about baseball and football and in return, he taught me the five-fingers discount. "Cut holes in your coat pockets and the stuff can drop into your lining," he told me on the second Saturday in November, turning his coat pockets out to show me the gaping holes he had in them. "If they're little, drop two on the floor. Put one back and the other in your sock."

About halfway through fifth grade is when I got the courage to steal. We were in Shaler's Pharmacy in the candy section when I saw an Apple Stix I wanted. I did not have a nickel at the time. Marshall encouraged me to go for it. I must have looked around a dozen times before I blindly snatched one and shoved it in my holey pocket. Nobody noticed. Not even Marshall. I could feel sweat under my armpits. All of a sudden, I got feverish and light-headed. "Let's get out of here," I whispered to Marshall. Marshall was staring at some strawberry licorice. "Wait a minute. I wanna pick up a few things," he said.

"I'll wait for you outside," I told him and made a break for the front door. The blue-eyed girl behind the front counter didn't even notice me leave. She was looking at some magazine, playing with her hair.

I waited for Marshall around the corner, out of sight. It was kind of cold. What my father would call "crisp." I wanted Marshall to make me feel better about what I had done. He tried. It didn't work. I have not stolen anything since.

July 2, 1964

Since nothing special is going on in my life right now, I might as well write about something that happened to me not long ago. There is this girl I like. She goes to my school. The last week of school, she wrote me a note telling me how much she liked me. On the last day of school, I got enough courage to tell her how much I liked her. Unfortunately, I have not seen her for a while because she has been away at her aunt and uncle's house in Cincinnati, Ohio. We write each other once a week (Actually, I write her a letter every day. I only mail them once a week). Judging by the size of her letters, I bet she does the same thing. She is supposed to be back tomorrow. I cannot wait.

On the way to Miller Park, Marshall and I always walk past her house. Marshall knows I like Fredrika. He was always trying to get me to talk to her but I couldn't. Every time I walked up to her, all I could say was "Hi!" After that, my mind would shut down. My mouth got dry as sawdust and my palms would sweat. When Fredrika smiled, talked, and asked me questions that only made things worse. When she smiles, I get lockjaw. When she talks, I listen to every word, and when she asks me questions, all I usually say is yes, no or maybe.

I talked to my parents about her. Mom said not to worry. Mom said in time I would talk to her and let her know how I felt about her. Mom also said that I was too young to get involved in any kind of "romantic relationship" with girls. Mom lost me with that one. If I am not supposed to get involved romantically with girls at my age, who am I supposed to get romantically involved with? I didn't dare ask mom that question. She would think I was trying to be smart.

Dad believed the same thing about my being too young but dad said not to concern myself with having a lot to say. "Just talk and more importantly listen," dad said. "And try to relax. She's a human being just like you. There is nothing to be afraid of."

On the last day of school, I took my father's advice. I felt a sense of urgency (where did I learn that phrase?). It was almost as if I would never see Fredrika again if I did not do something. I walked to school early and waited for her outside in the schoolyard. As soon as I saw her, I ran up to Fredrika and told her how pretty she looked and asked if I could walk her to class. I was scared. My heart was beating so hard I thought Fredrika could see it trying to bust out through my shirt. Her girlfriends were giggling. My partners, except Marshall, were laughing and pointing at me. I didn't care. I wanted Fredrika to know how I felt and I told her on that day. She was blushing a lot at the things that I said. That made me uncertain whether what I was saying was complimentary or silly. When I asked Fredrika if she wanted me to stop, she said no. She said she liked what I was saying. I almost lost it though, when she kissed me on the cheek before she went in for her first class. I got lockjaw again. I was just glad she had already gone inside the classroom and did not see me standing there looking stupid.

I walked Fredrika to every class. Most classes we had together. We held hands and talked. I was still nervous about doing or saying something dumb. The fellows made fun of me every chance they got, except Marshall. He was real. My parents were right. There was nothing to be afraid of about telling Fredrika how I felt.

July 3, 1964

Fredrika is supposed to be home today. She said she would call as soon as she got back.

July 5, 1964

I didn't hear from Fredrika yesterday so I called her. Her mom said she hadn't gotten home yet and would not be back until after ten o'clock tonight. I asked her if it would be okay for me to surprise Fredrika with a phone call in the morning. She said no it would not be okay and added she would tell Fredrika I called when she got home. I thanked her and hung up. I don't think Fredrika's mom likes me.

July 7, 1964

I hadn't heard from Fredrika so I didn't know if she had arrived safely, if something had happened, or if her mother hadn't given her my message. Marshall stopped by my house and we were on our way to Miller Park. On the way, Marshall asked me if I'd heard from Fredrika. I told him about the letters and that she was supposed to be home today. He asked me if I called. I told him what happened. We were about a block away from Fredrika's house when Marshall tried to make me promise that I would go up to the door and ask to see Fredrika. I couldn't, what if her mother answered, or worse yet, her father? From what Fredrika told me about him, he might tear my head off if he sees me. But Marshall wouldn't quit. He told me if I didn't do it, he would spread the word about how big a chicken I was. I told him I didn't care. He said he would get three dudes to beat me up every day until I did it. Even though I knew he was bluffing, I told him I could handle it. No threat he made mattered more than the fear I felt of possibly facing Fredrika's parents. Until Marshall said, he would tell my parents about my stealing. I didn't believe him at first but Marshall can be strange. Sometimes he will do something like that if he thinks it is the only way to get you to do something that he honestly believes is in your best interest. All I knew was I couldn't take that chance. I fear no one more than my father when he's discovered I've done something wrong. Marshall made me promise and I kept it.

I rang the doorbell. (God I was scared!) Thankfully, Fredrika answered the door. She looked fantastic! She threw her arms around me and kissed me on the lips before I could say anything. I heard her mother ask who was at the door from somewhere unseen in the house. Fredrika told her it was me and said she would be back in a minute. She took me by the hand and led me away for a walk. We talked and walked all afternoon. I guess Marshall went to the park by himself because I didn't see him after Fredrika answered the door.

July 13, 1964

Fredrika and I are spending a lot of time together. We meet at Miller Park and walk and talk. I haven't played football, baseball or basketball since Fredrika came back. She says her parents don't like us seeing each other. They think we're too young. Fredrika says she doesn't care, she won't stop no matter what they say. I told her I felt the same way.

The fellows have stopped making fun of me. I guess they have gotten used to us like Marshall said would happen.

Sometimes we ride our bikes together or we catch a bus to go window-shopping downtown or to the zoo or museum or movies. We like a lot of the same books and movies and things. Fredrika even likes baseball and basketball, a little. I have taken on a newspaper route and am getting one dollar a week allowance for doing my chores. I am also trying to get a part-time job at Fontelli's Market near our house. Mom thinks I am a little young to have a job. Dad is all for it. Neither one of them wants me to go spending all of my money on Fredrika. I told my parents that Fredrika gets an allowance too, two dollars a week and that most of the time we put our money together. (Fredrika will not let me put more money in than she has to put in.) Then we do things we like. If we don't spend it, we put it in our "entertainment fund" for another day. The more time I spend with Fredrika, the less nervous I am. I still get lockjaw when she smiles or kisses me. Dad says I'll have to get used to it. Dad says mom still stops his heart every now and then, like she did when he first saw her. I know what he means.

July 16, 1964

Fredrika and I are magic together. We see each other every day. Yesterday we went to the library and took out two books. One was called "Selected Poems" by Gwendolyn Brooks. The other one was "The Dream Keeper and Other Poems," by Langston Hughes. We rode our bikes to Overton Park, found a quiet spot near a big maple tree, and read to each other. Fredrika smelled so good. The sun seemed to dance on her skin. I watched her as she read. I tried listening but I didn't hear much of what she said. Her voice was "like the harps of angels." I got that from one of the poems I read.

Last night something weird happened. I was lying in bed, with my hands behind my head, thinking about Fredrika. It was hot and humid. I could not sleep and was laying on top of the covers with just my pajama bottoms on. My windows were wide open and the curtains were tied back so some air could get in. Once in a while a breeze would come through. It didn't cool things off but it was nice.

I heard a baby cry. It was faint but I knew what it was. I thought about Camille. I tried to remember her: how she looked, how she sounded, her touch. The harder I tried the more difficult it got. Her image was distorted and fuzzy. I cried as quietly as I could. Tears kept coming so fast and big I could not wipe them away fast enough. I heard myself saying in a gargled voice, "I'm sorry Camille. I didn't know. Why couldn't you be still? I would have taken you out of the crib if you had waited. All you had to do was wait. Why couldn't you wait?"

When I woke up the air was cooler and the sun was out. I could still see some stars in the sky. I felt my baby sister's presence. I smiled. My body felt light and tired. I fell asleep. I really miss Camille.

August 3, 1964

The whole family is going to see my grandparents in Tarrant, Alabama. I don't like it. I love my grandparents. Normally I would be glad to go but I don't want to leave Fredrika. Fredrika doesn't want me to go either but says she understands. She promises to write like we did when she was in Cincinnati. I said I would do the same and that seemed to make us both feel better.

I haven't seen Grandma and Grandpa Johnson since I was eight. I don't remember much about them. Dad has some pictures of my grandparents and me together but they don't help much. I've talked to them on the phone and they seem very nice. I still wish I could stay here with Fredrika.

August 6, 1964

We made it. Dad drove the whole way. From the time we entered West Virginia all the way to my grandparents' house my parents were a little nervous. Seems some places we drove through were different from where we came from. I know that there are people who do not like us because we are Negroes. Organizations like the KKK and Nazis exist in Pittsburgh too. But I never realized that there were people that hated us so much they would actually hurt us. Why?

We got to my grandparents house without any problems. These are my father's parents. It turned out to be a family reunion. I got a chance to meet cousins, nieces, nephews, aunts, and uncles I never knew about. And they were from all over: Florida, Arkansas, California, Washington, Oregon, Massachusetts, Pennsylvania, Ohio, Maryland, Alabama, Tennessee, Missouri, and Virginia. Having all these relations is mind-blowing.

Some of us stayed at my grandparents' house. It is a very large house almost as big as a mansion. We were lucky enough to be one of those. Others stayed with family friends who seemed glad to "put them up." I also found out I do like my grandparents a lot. Just like my mom and dad said I would. I wish Fredrika were here.

August 10, 1964

Dinner was ready. We were having it picnic style in my grandparents' huge backyard. Mom asked me to go inside, wake Grandma up, and let her know it was time to eat. Grandma had gone upstairs to take a nap. She said she was tired.

I ran upstairs and tapped on Grandma's door. There was no answer. A white rectangle of light filled up the cracked opening of the door. I whispered into the light, "Grandma." There was still no answer. I pushed open the door slowly and walked in. The windows were open. There was a lot of sunlight coming from everywhere. Made her room bright and what my mom would call "airy," whatever that means.

I liked how it smelled. My grandparents have apple blossom and cherry blossom trees all over the front and back yards. Her room smelled like a sweet mixture of both. Grandma was lying on the far side of the bed with her back to me facing the windows. She was still wearing her flower dress and thick black shoes. I whispered louder, "Grandma, time to eat." Grandma did not answer. I crept up to the bed. Something real cold ran through me. It felt like somebody replaced all of my blood with ice water. I stared at Grandma's silver hair lying loose on the pillow, afraid to move, scared to touch her. Through the floor, I heard my grandfather, Uncle Ronald, and my dad laughing. I reached for her. My hand trembled. I shoved her shoulder then jerked back my hand and waited. Grandma did not move. With both hands, I reached for her and stopped. My body backed into the wall. *Grandma's not there*, I thought.

I slid along the wall. It was smooth. My hand found the open doorway. I ran down the stairs and into the dining room. "Grandma won't wake up!" I told my father with my Uncle Ronald and grandfather standing there listening. My grandfather looked worried. "What do you mean she won't wake up Gratey?" he asked me. I could not answer him. I looked around the room and everyone was staring at me. My little cousin, Gandee, came running in the back door being chased by his brother, Roosevelt. When they saw us, they stopped and stared at me too. They all looked at me like I had done something wrong and they expected an explanation. Dad moved to me and asked me the same thing his father had asked and I told him. "I shook Grandma and she won't wake up." Next thing I know someone put a hand on my shoulder. I turned so fast to see who it was I almost fell and it was Grandma. I hugged her so hard she said I was going to break her ribs. Then I started crying. I could not help it. She asked me why I ran out of the room like my pants was on fire. I told her I thought she was gone. Everybody seemed to understand why I freaked out after I said that and we went ahead and ate dinner. It took me a while to get over the embarrassment. I was just glad Grandma was all right.

August 18, 1964

We are home. Dad drove the whole way back. We were still nervous but not as much as when we had gone down there. We got home Saturday night; too late for me to call Fredrika. We unpacked, took turns taking a bath, ate a light dinner, and went to bed. I fell right to sleep. The whole reunion thing was fun.

August 19, 1964

Saw Fredrika today. We were both so excited to see each other we couldn't stop talking for two straight hours. I missed her so much I went right to her house this morning. Her father answered the door. He invited me in and asked me to have a seat while he went to get Fredrika. (She was in her room reading one of my letters she told me later.) When her father came back and sat down, I thought I was going to die. He asked me how I was. How my folks were doing and what Fredrika and I had planned for the day. And that was it. I could tell he was not happy by the way he stared at me like he was looking at someone he did not trust. It was only a few minutes but felt like a lot longer. When Fredrika came in the room, I was ready to leave. He asked us where we were going and we told him. He seemed satisfied, after he reminded Fredrika she had to be home by two to help her mom with dinner tonight. After Fredrika said she would, she kissed her father on the cheek and we left. I noticed something when she did that. Her father lit up just like I do when Fredrika kisses me.

We went to Miller Park, walked, and talked. I saw Marshall and some of the fellows. I talked to them for a few minutes, told them a little about the trip and how big my family was. Fredrika and I were holding hands the whole time. They asked me if I wanted to play basketball and I told them not now, maybe later. I didn't mean it. I wanted to spend every moment with Fredrika.

September 7, 1964

Tomorrow school starts. I asked Marshall if he had been keeping a summer diary. He said "No chance." I asked Fredrika if she had been keeping one. She said she had. She offered to show it to me. I told her I didn't want to see it. If it's anything like mine, I think it's too personal to share with anyone. Not even Fredrika. I'm even having second thoughts about handing it in to Mrs. Bourgeault.

September 12, 1964

Mrs. Bourgeault gave us back our diaries yesterday. Most of the class had kept one. All of us that did got A's for half our written assignments for the entire year. We also do not have to do a final term paper.

Fredrika still tried to show me her diary. I would not look. The girls passed their diaries around to their girlfriends, reading them then commenting and laughing about things they had read. The boys kept their diaries to themselves. I stuck mine in my book bag and never let my book bag out of my sight. I was surprised Marshall did not ask to see it. Either he did not care or he already knew what my answer would be. Brian tried to take my book bag from me so he could read my diary. After I busted his lip, he stopped. None of the other fellows tried anything after that.

I'm never going to show anyone this diary. It's too personal. This is my last entry. I hate to write.

I heard the front door open. "Honey, come help me with the groceries!" I must've been so preoccupied with reading Gratey's diary I didn't hear the car pull up. I darted across the room, tossed Gratey's diary back into the open drawer, and slammed it closed. It was loud. I listened for a moment expecting Josephine to call to me. Ask me what I was doing. Not a peep came to my ears. As quickly as I could I tiptoed down the stairs.

From the living room window, I saw Josephine having straightened from lifting a bag of groceries from the back seat of our car. She was wearing a cool white sundress. The one I always told her complimented her healthy figure. Time had added a few pounds, a couple of wrinkles and streaks of noble gray. As Josephine walked along our sunlit path, I saw a woman still blessed with grace and power and innate beauty . . . my Ethiopian queen . . . my African bride . . . for whom I humbly opened the door and relieved of her burden.

STORY THIRTEEN

My father as a young man
-- The Prophet

When I returned home, October fifth of '68, it was not what I expected to be returning to. In all honesty, I wasn't sure what would be waiting for me. Maybe expected was the wrong word. "Hoped" would have better described my outlook.

What I'd hoped for was a ticker-tape parade, fanfare, applause . . . elaborate celebrations that would emphatically state America was proud of what we'd done, and welcomed us safely home. What we got were long-haired freaks wearing peace symbols and tie-dyed clothes, throwing shredded American flags and burning draft cards in our faces . . . spitting at us . . . calling us murderers and child molesters.

That really pissed off some of the vets. A few got into fistfights, shouting matches, spit back. Compared to what we'd been through, that protest shit was minor league as far as I was concerned. I only wanted to go home.

Debriefing was quick and painless. Army Doc looked me over. He treated me for mono and some other shit I can't remember. Was supposed to see the dentist but for one reason or another that never happened. Army shrink asked me a few "standard questions" off this sheet of paper he had on a clipboard. Guess he was trying to find out if I was fit to reenter society. A couple of weeks later, I was on a plane to Pittsburgh.

Home.

I hadn't told my parents I was back. When mom opened the door, she was flabbergasted. She and dad took turns hugging me until my body felt numb. Dad held me at arm's length, surveying me, like some cherished stolen heirloom returned in one piece. I did little more than hug them back and offer -- what I will now call -- a painful smile more for how it felt rather than how it looked.

Dad hadn't changed much. His dark skin was as smooth and shiny as ever. His hair, salt and pepper when I had left, was all gray and his little paunch had swollen into prominence. Still he was the beardless, pleasant, smiling man in the photograph I had carried in my wallet of him and mom in front of our house.

Everyone who knew my father as a young man says I strongly resemble him. When I looked at his face, into his soul, I searched for the resemblance. Moist brown mirrors reflected a sensitive and firm vision of me gazing at myself. It would be only the second time I'd ever see my father cry. The first being when Camille died.

Mom was a different story. Age was clearly her nemesis. She had become a plump, somber woman, with eyes that seemed too large for their lids. Her face was lined downward in a fashion that was testimony gravity does exist. Mom admitted she had put on weight and dad agreed, but it wasn't her weight that concerned me.

What I hadn't realized until dad told me during one of our walks is that mom blamed herself for Camille's death. She believed if she had the crib bars higher, Camille would not have been able to do what she did.

Dad said he told mom it was his fault. He believed he should have moved the crib into their room since Camille was prone to be less active when she could see her parents. Then Camille might not have attempted to climb out.

No matter what they said, or thought, I knew who was to blame. Camille was under big brother's care and I failed.

After Camille died, the mood of our home changed. We didn't say much to one another. Eye contact was minimal. Not once did we talk about the funeral or mention Camille's name.

Don't get me wrong. I can't remember a single incident when my parents made me feel to blame for what happened. There was no sense of being less loved or appreciated. I suppose you could say we were a family in limbo. Camille had left a huge crater we didn't know how to fill. We needed a way back to the way it was before Camille died. We were all searching for a means back to each other.

Dad gathered up all of Camille's things, the crib, Pepper, everything (except a few black-and-white photos), and gave them away to the Goodwill. That was his way of purging himself of her memory, I suppose. Mom stayed busy around the house, kept a summer garden, took up needlepoint and knitting, and became more active in community and church organizations. My way was to become the best damn son I could be for them.

I became a permanent honor-roll student. I was elected president of the Student Union my senior year. Joined the chess club, debate team, yearbook committee, prom committee, student activities committee, and graduated class valedictorian. On top of that, I held down a part-time job at "Cleavon's Soul Cuisine." I started out as dishwasher, worked my way up to busboy, finally becoming headwaiter in less than two years. Other parents lectured their children on how they "should try to be more like that Johnson boy." And so it went.

It helped. My parents were proud of their son. But the crater remained fixed in our lives. An abyss canvassed under a coarse blanket of self-denial. Now and then, it would expose itself, a bolt of memory, a careless word about her smile, her laugh, her smell, her touch. A dream turned nightmare when you awoke and she was not there. We kept busy, lied to each other, and to ourselves, that things were okay. We learned to live the lie.

There were times after Camille's passing, both in the years before I was drafted and the years after my return, I'd find mom alone, reflective, silent tears marking her mournful face. When she'd notice me (I probably had one of my pitiful faces on, which didn't help), mom would hastily smear the tears across her cheeks with the backs of her hands, pretending it was the movie -- if the television was on, or memories of her dad, whom she worshipped, if it wasn't.

Strange thing about tears, they're distinguishably different. There are tears for elation, physical pain, fear, anger, depression, relief, disappointment, anguish, and permanent loss. I had seen all shapes and brands fall from my mother's eyes. The ones she shed, for the supposed movie or memory of her father, were the same ones she shed at her only daughter's funeral. The same ones she periodically shed for the remainder of her life.

Mom made my favorite dinner the night of my return: baked ham with pineapple, collard and mustard greens, cornbread, candied yams, and for dessert, homemade cherry pie. Wolfed it down so fast I almost vomited.

All the time I felt like I was being watched. They asked if I felt okay, if anything was wrong. "Nothing far as I can see," I told them. But dad wouldn't let go. Kept insisting something wasn't right. Until my mother told him, "Leave the boy alone. He's just tired from all of that war nonsense."

I agreed with mom. Dad didn't, I could tell. For mom's sake, he let it go . . . for the time being.

STORY FOURTEEN

On the threshold of tears
-- Carrie Alyssa Washington

"Carrie if you really want to succeed at General Electric, learn company politics, listen to the people that know and give up that whining broad routine."

"Kiss my ass, Darwin."

"Now that's the spirit!" Darwin turned from the brightly colored blouses and eyed a nearby rack of solids.

"Which one do you like?" Darwin held up two blouses, one a deep V, powder blue with aqua trimming, the other a solid scarlet with an upturned collar. Carrie eyed each blouse thoughtfully. "The blue one," Carrie said.

"Me too," Darwin said.

"What difference does it make?" Carrie said. "They're not going to have your size. They don't make women's clothes large enough to fit your big ass."

Darwin hung the scarlet blouse back on the rack, and then held the blue one against his armor-plated, T-shirted chest. He critiqued himself in a small rectangular mirror hanging from a thin wire above the rack. The girl behind the women's accessories counter rolled her fawn eyes at the spectacle.

"Oh what the hell," Darwin flippantly said with a sassy wiggle of his slender waist that had taken him years to perfect. "I'll make one. Those picnicking fools will be so drunk they won't notice what I'm wearing."

"They won't notice a six-four black man, wearing make-up, a wig, pumps, a leather skirt, and a blouse? Where do you work at The Blind Institute?"

113

Darwin wrinkled his nose at Carrie. "You knew I was kidding," he said, a thread of irritation in his baritone voice. "I would never be in drag at my company's picnic."

"Pants, pants, maybe I'll get a pair of jeans while we're here?" Darwin said, with his left forefinger lightly inserted into the dimple of his chin and his right hand resting daintily on his waist.

"Darwin, you got a cigarette?" Carrie asked.

"I don't smoke -- you know that, and you shouldn't either." Darwin looked smug. "Carrie, there's something I've always been meaning to ask you."

"What?"

"How'd you come to realize you were gay?" Darwin said.

"I'm not gay," Carrie said. "I'm a lesbian."

"Forgive me," Darwin said. "I didn't know there was a difference."

"Homosexual men are gay," Carrie said. "Since men derived the term it's been adopted by the homosexual community. Just like everything else in a male-dominated society, men dictate how things are implemented and defined."

"Save it Carrie, I'm on your side, and you're evading the question. Why did you turn on to women?"

"Why'd you turn on to men?"

Carrie looked up at Darwin, her narrow clean face taut as a drum, her thin, plucked eyebrows pressing hard into the crest of her tiny nose. "Damn cigarettes," she said under her breath.

"You know darn well --," Darwin began before Carrie interrupted.

"It was that sweet child Jeremy. You were sixteen and never had the slightest sexual interest in men. Jeremy opened your eyes -- not to mention other parts -- helping you to see the light. I know all that."

"Why ask?" Darwin said.

"That's who, not why."

There was a pause. Carrie was in no mood for Darwin's bullshit and he knew it. She looked at him with her steely brown eyes that could manacle his coyness.

For Darwin this was when the fun began. He loved making people angry, not to the point of physical violence, but to verbal hysteria. Something he had tried for years to accomplish with Carrie. In an arrogant gesture, Darwin tilted his head back and opened his mouth to speak, but stopped. Carrie appeared stunned, as if she had seen a corpse come back to life.

Darwin followed her line of sight. A tall, anorexic man with a thick, nappy beard and dull swarthy tangles of twisted hair approached them. His mahogany face had two badly healed scars that appeared the results of deep cuts made by a crude, jagged object. His lips were severely cracked and his stark, glazed eyes floated in a red labyrinth of countless veins.

He was the sort of man Darwin would normally have given a contemptuous frown. But there was something about him, this apparent derelict that uprooted pity. Something that made Darwin want to take him by the shoulders and inject into his psyche the promise that no matter what he'd been through, it would be all right in the end. Whatever unearthed this compassion, dismantled his time-honed defenses, Darwin forced to the forefront his central credo in dealing with his type . . . caution.

The man stopped directly in front of Carrie, his sad eyes marveling her stunned face.

"Hi Carrie," the words seemed an accident. His voice was hoarse like a man just awakened from a deep sleep. His breath smelled like vomit and vinegar. Carrie stared, not flinching, astonished, and making an attempt at an ill-fated smile.

Darwin watched curiously, took a quiet step backward, hoping to become inconspicuous enough to be noticed but not obtrusive. A teenage couple pointed at the derelict and whispered as they walked by. A man in a business suit and a woman in a white summer dress frowned disapprovingly at the forsaken soul. Darwin caused the two of them to scurry with an unmistakable don't-fuck-with-me look.

Carrie asked the stranger how he was. He said fine, and then reached for her face with ashen palms. Darwin fought an urge to intervene. *She doesn't need to be rescued*, he thought although he could not justify his reasoning.

The stranger's hands stopped short of Carrie's face by the diameter of a quarter. Carrie stepped backward and glanced at Darwin. Her eyes wavered in confusion.

The man backed away from Carrie, looked blankly at Darwin, and then as quietly as he appeared, he left through one of the revolving glass doors on the far side of the store. Darwin wasted no time. Darwin stepped up to Carrie as if lost, desperately seeking directions. "Who was that?" he asked.

Carrie mumbled something into Darwin's chest having surprised him with a gripping hug. Her face had turned toward the accessories girl, who had condemnation stenciled all over her made-up face. Normally, Carrie would have accosted her with her biting wit. But the stranger had arrested that quality.

"What's wrong honey?" Darwin said. Darwin was hugging her. People were gathering, staring, whispering.

With a distinguishable quiver in her voice Carrie said, "Let's get out of here."

In her white cotton slacks, sleeveless sweatshirt, and low-cut canvas tennis shoes with no socks, Carrie was common. What would be considered "normal" by the society at large. But Darwin demanded attention as he followed her through the store. He exaggerated the swivel of his waist, switched his powerful hips, and made conscious shoulder and arm movements to exhibit his self-proclaimed femininity.

Carrie never looked back. She was not aware of the gawks and hushed remarks aimed at Darwin. Carrie focused her being on leaving the store through the same revolving doors as did the stranger.

They emerged into a sun-bleached, sluggish world. The throng that existed when they entered Kaufmann's had stemmed to a flowing pulse. Carrie's transition was swift. A moment ago, Darwin believed Carrie on the threshold of tears. Now her eyes were those of the brash, confident woman Darwin had come to respect and love, but not understand.

Two short steps to Carrie's left stood a comatose old man. She paid no more attention to The Prophet than she did to the streetlights at each corner.

Darwin could tell Carrie wanted to talk. She always behaved this way when she had something meaningful to say. Darwin moved from her right side and stood directly in front of Carrie. Carrie continued staring to her left. Darwin stroked her cheek with the smooth back of one of his large hands. Carrie resisted the urge to slap his hand away. *He's only trying to help*, she thought.

"I can't believe how bad he looks," Carrie said.

Darwin dropped his hand letting it come to rest on her thin arm, the same arm that had deposited the straw bag on the ground near her feet. Her small round head leaned back against the display window. Darwin glanced over the top of her short Afro and noticed an anemic mannequin, wearing oval sunglasses and a multicolored one-piece bathing suit, posed in a way that reminded him of the children's song, "I'm A Little Teapot."

"That man," Carrie began abruptly. Darwin nodded a kindly affirmation. "He was my boyfriend in the eleventh grade. His name is David Carlson. Of course, everyone called him Dave."

Carrie paused and looked up into Darwin's powerful face. "I loved him so much. Don't really know why -- he wasn't great looking. He looked a lot better then than he does now, but he was never the kind of boy that would make a girl giggle or whisper silly things about him as he walked past. He wasn't smart or athletic. Truthfully, Dave was far too often an outright fool, and I fell in love with him. So far in fact I got pregnant."

"Is he the one you had the abortion for?"

"Yep, well, sort of," Carrie said. "Dave didn't know about the pregnancy -- or the abortion until it was over."

"You never --" Darwin stopped and looked around as if to make certain no one was eavesdropping, "you never told him you were pregnant?" he eventually whispered.

"No," Carrie said. "Like I said I loved him, but I didn't think he was very bright. I thought he'd be happy . . . at least understand."

"I'm trying to understand myself, honey."

"I was only fifteen years old."

"You couldn't have gotten an abortion by yourself," Darwin said. "How'd your mother feel? What about your father?"

"Are you kidding?" Carrie said. "My mother made the arrangements. She couldn't wait to get it over with. I can still hear her infantile voice: 'It's all for the best sweetie. You'll understand when you get older.' I still ain't old enough."

Carrie looked around in disgust. Her glance stopped at The Prophet. He seemed to have moved closer.

"My father, now there's an understanding man," Carries said. "When he found out I was pregnant, he became furious. Yelled and swore at me, beat my mom, all the time talking about it was her fault, and she believed him. He called me a whore. Made it very clear, my bastard child and me wouldn't live one day under his roof. I couldn't believe it. I went from his baby girl to a slut just like that." Carrie snapped her fingers. "He wouldn't even talk to me about it."

Carrie stared fiercely at The Prophet. "I'll never forgive my father for slapping me. When I needed him most, my daddy washed his hands of his only child."

Darwin watched Carrie as she watched The Prophet.

Carrie recognized The Prophet as the man she had described to a girlfriend as "this wild fool, wearing crazy clothes, yelling at people about God." He appeared not to be breathing. Quiet, still. How many times had Carrie laughed at him? How many times had she made fun of this lunatic preacher, self-deluding himself into saving defiant souls? What about his soul Carrie wondered. Who assured his salvation?

"Before I worked up the courage to tell Dave about the abortion, he found out from his friend, Booke," Carrie said. "Booke was a football player. They called him Backbreaker Booke in those days. Dave worshipped the ground this dude walked on, and for some odd reason, Booke really dug Dave. Even though they were the same age, it was as if Booke adopted Dave as his kid brother. Booke wouldn't let anybody fuck with Dave, not even his teammates. Word around Salvation was, you messed with Dave, and you had to deal with Backbreaker.

"How'd Booke find out about my abortion? I haven't the slightest idea. So what do you think Dave does?"

Darwin stared ruthfully at Carrie.

"Dave asks me to marry him," Carrie said. "Can you believe that shit? I couldn't. Being young and dumb, I said yes."

"Carrie, you can stop here if you want," Darwin said.

"Why?" Carrie asked.

Darwin had no answer.

"February 17," Carrie said. "I remember the date exactly. It was ten days after Dave asked me to marry him and six days after my birthday. Dave helped Booke, or Booke helped Dave, rob a grocery store. The police chased them. Their getaway was a stolen car. They took out a telephone pole trying to escape. Booke got a couple of broken bones, some minor cuts, but otherwise, he was okay. Dave came away with all sorts of injuries: broken ribs, cracked clavicle, sprained knee, bumps, bruises, lacerations. The child was a mess. Dave said he did it for us, so we'd have a little cash for a wedding. Ain't that a fool for you? He wants to begin our *mat-ri-monial* lives with stolen money."

Darwin watched Carrie who appeared composed and reflective. He could tell Carrie was solidly in control.

"To make a long story short, they were convicted. Booke got three years. Dave got five to ten. Guess Backbreaker had connections."

Carrie looked Darwin squarely in his eyes. "He was only seventeen years old."

Her sigh was heavy, unloading an ancient burden onto the gray sidewalk before Darwin's feet.

"When I walked out of that courtroom, I never looked back. I left home, school, everything. Just said, 'fuck it' and walked away. End of story."

Darwin hugged her. When Carrie shoved Darwin away, he realized he'd made a mistake.

"Why don't we," Darwin whispered into her ear, "go to Baskin-Robbins and get a couple of pistachio sundaes, my treat."

"Feeling sorry for me," Carrie said. "Expecting me to cry? Fall apart?"

"You know sorry ain't my thing babe," Darwin said.

"Don't patronize me! Only weak people cry. The strong know stuff like this is just a part of life, sweetheart." Carrie pinched Darwin's cheek. Darwin grinned. "Take this brother over here for example," Carrie said.

Darwin looked at The Prophet then immediately back at Carrie.

"Could've ended up like him," Carrie said.

"I doubt it," Darwin said.

"Why?"

"I could never see you in galoshes."

STORY FIFTEEN

Fear is your constant companion
-- The Prophet

In the field, fear is your constant companion. It eats, sleeps, laughs, and survives with you. It doesn't go away at the end of a firefight, ambush, flight home. It hangs on, burns out a spot in your brain to breed and manifest itself in rage or bitterness or unwarranted violence toward those who want to understand and love you.

My nightmares nursed that fear. Shelling me with visions so vivid I could feel the anxiety and despair, smell the NVR, gunpowder, rotted flesh. Hear those damn AK-47's and M-16's all over again, kicking back and forth. It got so I was afraid to close my eyes because when I opened them, I expected to find myself back in 'Nam.

There was one nightmare that occurred at least three times a week. It was the worst of them all. I called it "Village Of The Damned." It's the only nightmare I still have. While not as frequently as before, enough that it remains disturbing.

It begins with me hacking my way through thick underbrush. There is no danger. I know this. The same way I know I had taken the machete I was using from a dead VC. My M-16 is slung over my shoulder, safety on but ready to rock 'n' roll. In this place, I am known as Hun, the merciless one, the one to be feared first and foremost. With me, I bring something I think of only as "The Curse." Instinctively, I know what that means and smile to myself about it.

Suddenly I come upon a peasant village. Nothing special about it -- that's exactly what I think in the dream, "Nothing special about this village." For some reason I get it into my head to destroy it. I make my way around the perimeter and locate the best point of penetration. I notice how all the people walk with rigid movements as if their joints are frozen. Their faces are shallow with blank eyes that stare straight ahead. Blisters and open sores cover their stomachs, backs,

121

chests, legs, and arms. Some have limbs missing. Others have holes in their bodies you can see clear through. None of this seems strange to me. It is as expected.

I slip in behind this one straw hut on the outer edge of the village. It feels deserted. I mean exactly that, feels deserted. In the dream, I only sense this but it is as certain to me as if I'd looked inside. This disappoints me, makes me angry.

Like wartime, I go in low and slow, grenade ready in my left hand, M-16 ready in my right. I maneuver my way to the center hut of the village, undetected, before I throw the grenade. I think of this as demolishing the heart of this place.

After that, it's Hell's bells. Single-handedly, I launch an attack on that village, trying to obliterate everyone and everything.

No one screams or panics. No one cries, hollers, or runs. They keep walking as if I don't exist.

I continue my assault not at all surprised at their lack of reaction. The whole thing has me feeling exhilarated. Then, for no reason, I stop. I look around. All the people are gone, vanished, no bodies, no remains. Not a damn thing left standing in that place except one hut. The same hut I had sensed was empty.

I reload my rifle; trudge over to the hut, and am about to step inside when someone grabs me by the back of the neck. I whirl, ready to fire. My father and mother are standing there, holding hands, shaking their heads no. I half smile. They weep. I quickly turn and enter the hut. Camille is crawling on the packed dirt floor. She is happy, smiling, showing off her two teeth. She reaches for me and clearly says my name. I smile at her. In the next instant, I raise my rifle and fire. Then I wake up.

****

It didn't register about being scared I mean, until one calm, sunny Thursday.

I had gotten my job back as headwaiter at Cleavon's Soul Cuisine, my fifth job in as many months. My father invited me to go with him to his favorite neighborhood bar, Little Louie's, to celebrate. Since Little Louie's was only a block and a half from our house, we walked.

Things had changed quite a bit in my neighborhood in my absence. I don't deny it was a slum when I left, but it wasn't nearly as bad as it had become. There were punks hanging out on practically every street corner, looking ready to kill somebody. They didn't fool me. They were just as scared as I was. The only difference being their battlefield was urban, not jungle.

On the way to Louie's, dad and me ran into Ernie and Tony, a couple of my old-time hanging partners. They had gone to 'Nam a year before I did. Ernie was in a wheelchair, looking pissed off at the world and smelling as if he was still in the bush. Tony appeared to be okay, until you started talking to him and he'd space out.

Even as a kid, Tony would space out on you. His eyes would roll back just a little. That fat face of his get real relaxed. Then (once the vision was completed I always assumed), a tiny smile would turn up the ends of his narrow lips. I loved it, man. Look like pure heaven where that boy was. We nicknamed him "Spacey" because he did it so often. Teachers used to fry his behind for it. "How do you expect to learn anything when you're always daydreaming?" Mr. Denny would ask him. But Tony didn't care, kept right on doing it.

That time, and every other time I saw Tony after that day, he looked scared . . . of himself.

Up until that point in my life I had only gone to Louie's to fetch my father for my mother when I was a kid. So it was in the respect of a legal-aged man, a coming of age experience.

Only a handful of people were there. My dad called them "The Regulars." The front and back metal doors were wide open so the afternoon sun helped strip away the bland decorum of the bar. Clean and quiet with a pinch of chlorine bleach in the air. That's probably the best way to describe it.

Dad ordered us a couple of beers and a couple of shots of Jim Beam. We killed the shots and chased them with the beers to cool the inferno in our throats. Then he ordered another round.

We talked mostly about small stuff: changes in the neighborhood, who was sleeping with who, what businesses closed down, who was dead; stuff like that. We got quiet for a bit after we threw down the second shot. A pause for thought you might say. Then my father hit me with a bulldozer of a question: "What do you remember about Vietnam?"

I didn't react at first. I couldn't. There was nothing to comment on. It happened, a nightmare with my eyes opened and I survived. What was there to say?

I stared at my dad. He stared back. He looked as nondescript as I felt. I could relate to that. My dad was a sergeant during the Korean War, which made me understand his curiosity, and the lack of reaction on his face at the time.

Still, I couldn't figure out what was going on. *Maybe he was getting at something by asking me this*, I had thought. *Some shrink shit, or one war vet to another war vet bull session.* All I had done since I got back was try to forget. I would have thought he of all people would understand that. But all he did was keep his cool and stare.

I sat my beer down on the bar, turned on my bar stool a little, and looked around. There wasn't much to see. There were a couple of elderly people at separate tables nursing their drinks. A woman propped against the unplugged jukebox staring at the ceiling, gripping a bottle of RC cola in her slender hand. In the farthest corner, sitting in the deepest shadows of Louie's, was Mr. Duncan. Everybody knew him. Once a respected grade school teacher, he had become kind of the neighborhood wino if there's such a thing. Why did it happen to him? Who knows? I wanted to feel sorry for him but I couldn't. The best I could muster was apathy, which ain't a feeling at all.

My father waited while he sipped his beer. He didn't as much as grunt or sigh. "Patient as a stone," my mother would have said if she were there.

I stared back at my dad for a minute before this rush of hot anger ran all through me. It was as if someone turned up a furnace full blast in my gut, and then the furnace doors blew off and I swelled until I felt I was going to burst open. When it came out, it was me giving this bitter, angry summary, as if someone punched a hole through the center of my pain and released it.

"I can remember" -- that's how I began, staring at the Stroh's sign behind the bar, not really seeing it -- "humping across sun-scorched land, through swamps, into thick suffocating jungles; hauling seventy-five ball-busting pounds on my aching, blistering back. Night blackness so dense you couldn't see the sweat on your hands in front of your face; Slick, Daryl, Taylor, and the rest of The Brothers. A Saigon bargirl called herself Aunt Tootie. Smoking dope, beaucoup firefights, malaria, dysentery, razor-sharp elephant grass, bush sores, jungle rot, C-rations, snakes, scorpions, rats, blood-sucking leeches, fire ants, poisonous centipedes, weeks to months without a shower or clean fatigues, grown men crying, praying, scared, killing . . . dying inside . . . coming home.

"I saw a mountain of men die. Seen them blown-up, mutilated, skinned alive, and shot in places you never thought a human being could be shot. It got so you accepted it. You expected it to happen to you at any time, only vowing to go down clawing and scratching every inch."

I felt compelled to look at my father, to try to get a handle on what he was thinking. When I read in his eyes the silent confirmation only another combat veteran could comprehend, I realized immediately, I hadn't told him anything he didn't already know.

"Once you've been to hell dad what's left?"

I looked around again. The woman who was propped against the jukebox had sat down at the table in front of her, staring at her drink. No one else had changed position or expression. Life went on. I felt my father pat me on the back. His eyes were moist again. "Let it go son," was all he said.

STORY SIXTEEN

In the thick heart of summer
-- Nathaniel Jonathan Booke

"Ty! Better give up the rock, homie, or it's mine," a quick-footed defender wearing a red handkerchief around his neck boasted.

"Kick it!" yelled Ty's hanging partner, Cliff, who was running full speed down the left sideline.

Ty faked a one-handed pass to Cliff while keeping his dribble alive. Sneakers squeaked, slid, and pounded against the thirsty concrete as ten sweaty men demonstrated perpetual motion. Ty slashed by his badgering defender, after he froze him with a wicked head and shoulder fake, and swished in a jumper from the foul line.

"Bust him, Ty!" Booke yelled from the sideline. Ty raised a fist in quick salute, and then shadowed a squat teenager dribbling the ball up court.

In the thick heart of summer, the Miller Park regulars played at an all-out attack mode. The way they believed basketball should be played. Booke watched patiently from the sideline, talking with Charley and Herman about women and sports. His was the next game, and Charley and Herman were assured places on his team.

A kid wearing a black denim jacket, unlaced high-top sneakers, and wrinkled baggy corduroy pants walked hurriedly through the basketball court. He stopped at the far corner of the basketball court, as if in recognition of an invisible forbidden boundary, and waved at the group of three.

Booke noticed him first and nudged Herman who nudged Charley. The kid nervously smiled and waited, shuffling his feet from side to side. The men looked at each other in dismay, and then stared back at the kid. The kid pointed at them. The men continued to stare.

It took a minute before Booke realized who he was. He had not seen him since that one time, about nine months ago.

126

"Excuse me, fellows," Booke said as he started around the perimeter of the basketball court to avoid interfering with the game. Herman grabbed Booke by one of his thick forearms.

"You're not really going to sell that kid some shit are you?"

"If he got the scratch, damn right," Booke said, "this is business, you know how it is."

"I never sell to kids," Herman said.

"You ask for ID?" Booke said.

"You know what I mean."

Booke got within kissing distance of Herman. Herman looked down into his eyes, steady and poised.

"Herman's rules, you limit your clientele to people who can't afford to buy their families food, or pay the rent on some dump you wouldn't let your roaches live in."

"Bullshit," Herman said. "Most of my customers make more lettuce than you'll ever see."

"That explains why you always doing business in The Projects," Booke said.

"At least I ain't peddling around high schools," Herman said.

"When have you ever seen me doing my shit at a high school?" Booke said.

"That wasn't your red 'vette I seen in front of Salvation the other day?"

"I was picking up my little brother, and you know it."

Herman completely ignored Booke's answer. "Next you'll be hustling grade schools, like some of those sorry-ass unethical fuckers."

"Unethical," Booke scoffed. "Do you even know what the word means? What about that girl, Herman, the one whose jaw you broke last week. How old was she?" There was a pause, "eighteen, nineteen, twenty-one?"

The sound of Booke's voice sunk to an acid quality, eroding Herman's righteous resolve. Herman ground his teeth.

"And for what, huh, Herman; twenty dollars wasn't it?"

Booke paused. The skin on his face had become hot and tight. Anger was something he could not afford. It clouded his judgment, made violence his only recourse. A few deep, concentrated breaths made him steady but not calm. That would take time.

Booke scanned Herman's burning eyes, and then poked him in the center of his chest with a staunch finger.

"Big business man," Booke said indignantly. He paused. His voice instinctively became subdued, maintaining that severely hostile tone.

"Don't you ever play high and mighty with me again," Booke said. "You're no better than I am."

A roar of congratulations came from the players of one team after a lanky, balding man, nicknamed Weasel, made a jumper from the right corner.

Charley had taken a few casual steps to his right, absently staring at the baseball field at the other end of the grassy park. Herman turned his head and crossed his arms over his chest. "Fuck you," Herman said in a low, bitter voice. Booke stepped back and grinned. *You stupid son-of-a-bitch*, he thought, *we're both in so deep with this bullshit we might as well be hooked ourselves.*

Booke gave a low grunt in Herman's direction, glanced over at Charley, and then jogged across the temporarily vacated area of the basketball court.

"Hey Booke," the kid's voice was abnormally high-pitched and shaky. His breath smelled like Limburger cheese and his teeth were a sickly compound of green, gray, and yellow. Booke turned his head away from the kid and looked toward the parking lot, his back to the basketball court.

"What do you want?" Booke asked.

"Umm," the kid lowered his eyes. His voice dipped to a breathy whisper, "You got any stuff?"

This was not the boy Booke remembered from nine months ago. That kid had a cocky manner and an air of predestined success. The type of child you can look at and envision as a lawyer or doctor or Wall Street executive. When Booke asked him (in a moment of weakness) if he was sure he wanted to buy some crack, the boy had said, "No problem, no sweat." Booke believed him. *A thrill seeker, only curious about the high*, Booke had thought. Maybe this one,

Booke had speculated, would be too smart to play this game more than once.

The kid's eyes were bloodshot and murky. A deep bruise spotted the tan skin of his forehead. There were burns on the bridge of his nose and just below his bottom lip. He had seen faces like his on veteran consumers, people who had purchased chemical dreams for years.

"You got any money?" Booke asked.

The boy reached into his jacket pocket. Booke grabbed him by the wrist. "Not here." Booke motioned with an upward jerk of his head, "Over there in the parking lot."

Booke looked around, not a Narc in sight. Herman still had his arms crossed. Charley stood next to him. Herman said something to Charley, who shook his head in agreement. *Fuck you too Herman,* Booke thought, and then followed the kid at a distance into the nearby parking lot.

Booke removed a canvas pouch, tied with a leather string, from under the spare tire in the trunk of his Corvette. He untied the pouch and randomly chose one of the clear, plastic packages (no larger than a sugar packet) with a dull white substance inside.

After Booke retied the pouch and stuffed it back beneath the tire, he slammed shut the trunk and held out in his open palm what the kid had come for. The boy reached for it. Booke snapped his hand closed before the kid could touch it.

"Money," Booke said. His eyes nailed to the face of the kid. Anxiously, the boy fumbled through his pocket and presented a crumpled mass of paper currency gripped in a raised right fist. He laid the money in the steady palm of Booke's other hand. Booke took the money as if it were contaminated. Something told him not to do it. Make up any excuse just don't sell this kid anymore crack cocaine.

Tears filmed the boy's eyes as he stared hungrily at the package. The kid rocked unconsciously back and forth. His hands fisted in his jacket pockets. "Here!" Booke said and shoved the crack at his face.

The child snatched the crack and held it up to the sun. He smiled, jubilantly thanked Booke, and then ran and jumped into a rusting, dent-riddled '79 LTD.

Booke looked toward the basketball court. Weasel made a lay-up. Charley and Herman laughed about something Charley had said. The laughter sounded maniacal and sadistic from that distance. At first, Booke believed it was him they had been laughing at. Then a strange thought spilled into his mind. *What if they were laughing at the kid? The kid and all those like him. The suckers, the small fry, leaping headlong into a mirrored pond, layered with quicksand and blood.*

He unlocked the door to his immaculate Corvette and eased into the black leather seat. It fit him like one of his mother's hugs. For a brief moment, Booke leaned back and enjoyed the experience before he reached into his glove compartment for a pair of Gucci sunglasses and his red leather Gucci driving gloves.

The car started in a cacophonous rush, instantly leveling to a melodious orchestra of mechanical harmony. Out of habit Booke turned on the radio. Immediately, he switched it off. *Same old shit*, he thought.

The LTD bolted by him and squealed hysterically onto Fifth Avenue. Suddenly Booke realized something as he watched the kid turn the corner. He never knew his name.

How he got to the Point, Booke could not recall. What was even more important was why he was there? It had never been a place of tranquility or contemplation for him. Sure, he had swum in the Monongahela, Ohio, and Allegheny a few times. It was the time he swam here, where the three rivers meet, that he remembered the most. It was his last.

It was an August day, similar to this one except the sun was not quite so bright and there was a constant breeze. Herman, Charley, Ty, Louie, Dave, and he had decided to take a dip to cool off from playing baseball for the last three hours. At the age of twelve it was common for them to strip to their underwear, once a week, and swim in the "fishy smelling" water in an effort to retard the energy-draining effects of the brutally hot, humid Pittsburgh summers.

There was a game they played similar to chicken in which they would see who could swim out the farthest. Herman always won. *This time, just maybe*, Booke had thought, *he might be able to defeat him.*

This was spirited by the fact Booke had hit his first home run, the winning home run, for their little league Redhawks.

With his eyes closed, Booke swam out determined that day the title would belong to him. A strong undercurrent seized Booke and he could not break free. He panicked, started screaming, splashing, swallowing water. Through water-filmed eyes, Booke could see the blurred riverbank moving away. Booke struggled harder, clawing for the surface each time the current dragged him under.

Dave swam out and saved him. He had to punch Booke in the stomach to calm Booke down so they both didn't drown.

Booke recovered on the concrete bank. Dave was the only one who asked if he was OK. The rest nervously watched and listened, as Booke coughed and vomited his way back to life.

Then there was quiet. They did not look at one another, but stared in reverence at the three rivers. It was as if the rivers were suddenly alive and it was Booke's brief tussle with death that made them aware of it.

Booke did not feel vengeance, anger, or bitterness in looking at the rivers. Instead, he harbored a sense of awe beneath the chilling waves of shivering fear, a feeling that demanded his respect.

Fine mist dampened his face, neck, and hands. It felt cool, clean, and gentle. He turned to look at the fountain from where the mist was stolen. A huge jet stream of water shot into the clear air. Groups of people, young through middle-aged, wearing shorts or swimsuits, splashed, laughed, and waded through the dark pool of water at the circular, concrete basin surrounding the base of a large fountain.

If only the water could cleanse him. Relieve him of his mounting nausea. Wash away the sewer in his belly filtered only by his decaying conscience. Allow the last few years of crap he sold to steam away, like still water under a desert sun. And all the anguish and shadowy promises, bolstered by the substance of lies, seed transverse clouds, and rain upon fields where hope flowered into fulfilled dreams. Maybe then he could try again. Maybe Godfrey would see the difference and make a change in himself. Maybe that kid whose name he didn't know would . . .

On the rim of the basin walked a man whose beard and hair grew with untamed wills of their own. His smooth, swollen belly hung low over his urine-stained cotton shorts. His arms and bare chest were as skinny as the thin ribs threatening to poke through his constricted skin.

Shit, Booke thought, *not Dave. I don't feel like dealing with the brother right now.*

Booke stood and turned to leave. Gliding up river an empty barge peaceably made its way. The captain and his scanty crew waved to a small band of children on shore. The children excitedly pointed, waved, and yelled back to the crew. Booke sat down and stared at the barge as if it were the last ship leaving this foreign land to take him home.

Booke watched the barge, the children, and the sunlight play upon the ripples of jade green water. The time of the near tragedy replayed in his fatigued mind. An occasional loud cough from him had jolted them into a forced acknowledgment of each other. Even then it was no more than an empty glance. Booke saw those rivers now, the way he saw them then. It made him wonder, what if he would have drowned.

STORY SEVENTEEN

Though As A Child
-- The Prophet

Gratey raised his weathered face from the damp wooden slats of a park bench, glints of clear dawn reflected in his swollen red eyes. His neck was stiff and ached. Before Gratey moved, his mind took a swift mental inventory of his condition. A reflex learned in combat: body parts, rigid, but functional; breathing: steady; heartbeat: regular.

He felt no leeches on his body or snakes or insects or rodents sharing his clothes. Gratey listened intensely for any unnatural sounds but heard none. His eyes were bleary but he managed to survey his surroundings. Nothing moved. Wherever Gratey was it was safe.

To the tune of grunts, groans, and faint sighs, he sat upright. With a sandpaper-coarse hand, he rubbed his face, and then casually looked around an area no larger than one city block on any side. After a moment of strained concentration, its name came to him, Smithfield Park.

They call this a park. Gratey found that thought amusing. Yet for him this place had provided one night's sanctuary. A refuge in the steel heart of his orphaned city nourished by timed water sprinklers and constructed of stone and gray marble and transplanted bushes and trees. A plot of land elevated two flights of steps from the downtown streets, removed and efficiently arranged to justify the dubbing park.

Though Gratey and his friends amused themselves through lustrous summer days in Smithfield Park as children, two questions popped into his mind: How'd I get here, and why?

Between Gratey and the bench to his immediate left was a garbage can. The kind gaudily disguised in stone stucco and capped with a tan metal hood. Gratey eased off the hood and placed it attentively on the ground. With the stealth of a night burglar, Gratey

133

carefully removed his duffel bag from inside, cursing under his breath at how heavy it was.

In a muffled clap, the duffel bag landed erect on the pavement in front of him. Gratey rested it on his thighs and briefly inspected its contents. Everything was neatly folded and tucked in place. Gratey brushed away the loose debris from his duffel bag with quick even sweeps, and then leaned it against the bench he had been sleeping on before he sat down.

Out of a distant sleep-fog, a murky recollection of a beat cop surfaced. The cop had said she would arrest Gratey for loitering if he were there when she returned. Little did the cop know leaving was Gratey's sole intent.

Gratey rubbed his face again and sighed. His head throbbed. The morning air felt cool and refreshingly damp on his dry skin. A stale, bitter taste made him spit. He searched the ground around the bench, no vomit anywhere. Gratey looked over the park again, still no one else there. He worshipped the solitude. Even in 'Nam moments like these were treasures. If ever a perfect world existed, it was in the tranquil, placid mornings of the jungle, before the first words were spoken and danger took a firm foothold in his consciousness. Before warring men invaded and destroyed its native splendor, when his surroundings seemed to give thanks for being allowed to exist one more day. A world suspended in grace under the omniscient eye of God.

Footfalls softly echoed from across the park. Gratey jumped to his feet and swung his duffel bag over his shoulder. He stumbled sideways before falling on his butt. Nausea and dizziness made standing intricate. The footsteps sounded closer. Gratey shook his head. Using the bench for support, Gratey methodically stood. Then, as quickly as his rubbery legs could carry him, he rushed to the nearest exit.

Gratey stared down the flight of steps leading to a landing. They seemed a burden he did not wish to tackle. A dot of sunlight, no larger than an orange, appeared near his feet. The sound of footsteps stopped. He breathed deeply. His nose began to run. The new air cleared his head, bottled his fear. "Hey you," he heard her yell. Gratey did not look back as he staggered desperately down the black marble steps leading him back to the streets.

****

Fredrika, her favorite color is chestnut, her favorite flower, love-in-a-mist. We watched sunrises together and witnessed overpowering red sunsets. On her sixteenth birthday, at the center of a sweaty August afternoon, we danced to Smokey Robinson and The Miracles, The Temptations, The Supremes, Gladys Knight and The Pips, and others music whose slow, sensual rhythms brought our bodies close. That same day, I gave Fredrika presents of her favorite flowers, a box of chocolates, and a silver locket with our pictures in it that she proudly wore from that time forward. We kissed, hugged, fondled, touched, unsure teenagers exploring foreign forms of physical expression. Her existence was my first real belief there was a God. Only a super being could make a woman that lovely, the sweetest of life's offerings, the most precious of gifts. I never felt so complete, so . . . in love in all my life. Why'd I have to fuck it up?

When I was drafted into the Army, we were engaged. My priorities had changed from when I was a child. College had become a far more serious consideration than the armed forces. I was enrolled at the University of Pittsburgh when I received my draft notice. For whatever reason, I felt it was my duty to comply. To be honest, I had little idea what was going to happen to me in the service. Guess I still had visions of combat glory marching around in my head. I bought into the trip of war being this simple, sterile game kids play and television and films glorifies. To me it felt no different from going away to an extended summer camp where boys became disciplined men, returning home older, smarter, and ready for the world. What a fool I was.

When my tour of duty was over and I got back to Pittsburgh, Fredrika was gone. Her parents had divorced. Mr. Booke still lived in their old house. I asked her father about his daughter. He wouldn't talk. He didn't like me any more than when Fredrika and I began dating back in middle school. Puckett -- an old high school buddy who stayed up on the neighborhood goings-on -- told me in his wordy manner, Fredrika had moved to Philadelphia.

I hadn't heard from Fredrika since I left the States. I assumed she was writing but the letters weren't getting through. That was common shit when you were stationed overseas, especially in a war zone. Mail was always being fucked-over, lost, or ripped off. Still, in the back of my mind, I had really hoped Fredrika would be there when I got back. Strange thing though, when Puckett told me about Fredrika being gone, all I could do was shrug my shoulders and muster an "Oh well."

Then Fredrika came back to visit her father. She told me she thought I was dead since I hadn't written her and no one else had heard from me. I told Fredrika that I had written a lot. Apparently, none of my letters got through. Fredrika made this lame joke about them floating around in our postal system waiting to be delivered. She thought it was hysterical. All I could do was shake my head and smile. Somehow, some way, I talked Fredrika into moving back to Pittsburgh. When she did, we tried picking up where we left off.

Physically Fredrika hadn't changed. The girl was still a natural baby-faced queen. When Fredrika smiled, it was as if she were a bashful child embarrassed at being noticed. Like a moonbeam creasing the darkest night you can imagine. Couple those qualities with a firm figure, soft smooth skin the color of liquid gold, and huge brown eyes and you got one gorgeous lady.

What had changed about Fredrika was positive. To her girlish charm, she had added grace, poise, articulation, and a self-assured maturity you'd expect to find in royalty.

It was clear to me we weren't the same people. Our high school romance seemed like a fantasy I had that never came true. My lady was all grown up. I, on the other hand, had blown a fuse.

I loved that woman. Always will. Still didn't stop me from whoring around, staying out late, getting drunk, fighting. There was this uncontrollable meanness in me I couldn't shake like those damn nightmares. Every time I tried to do the right thing something inside would make me do the opposite.

The shrink said I had a suicide wish. I told him he was full of shit. Ain't no way I'd go through all that crap in 'Nam to come home and try to kill myself. The shrink said that some people who are suicidal do it in one fell swoop. Others do it in stages. Mine was obviously supposed to be in the stage category. I don't know. The asshole could've been right for once.

Maybe that's why Fredrika would never marry me. She wouldn't come out and say it, but I'm sure she recognized I wasn't the same man she knew in high school.

Even after the kids were born, I couldn't change. Would take the money for their formula, clothes, diapers, what-have-you, and buy wine or smoke, and every once in a while, a cheap, back-alley whore.

But Fredrika stayed. I'll never understand why.

Actually, I stayed with her. She was the one who could keep a job. It's a wonder as many bosses I punched out I wasn't in jail. Fredrika took care of things, the house, kids, bills, me.

One day I woke up just as the sun angled through our bedroom window. For once, I didn't have a hangover. I took a hard look at Fredrika's face. Her skin was as dull as death. Across her forehead were lines cut deep and wide. Even with her face relaxed, Fredrika looked sad. I thought about the girl I danced with on her sixteenth birthday, made the comparison of then and now. What she'd become, I did to her, chipping away at her pride and character, resilience and faith. A woman I would have died for as a young man, I was murdering with my selfish, maniacal behavior.

I got up and kissed Fredrika on her forehead. She didn't twitch. I got dressed and looked into the kids' room. They were sleeping like stones. I was afraid to walk in, scared one of them might wake up and see me saying my silent good-byes.

I left the house and came back at about ten that morning. Fredrika was at work and the kids were in school. Packed my old army duffel bag with as many clothes could fit and split. Disappeared, vanished, had no plans of ever coming back, but it didn't work out that way.

****

I looked up from the seat I had dozed off in inside the Greyhound bus terminal. The ticket clerk eyed me warily. It was Sunday morning. The clerk had begrudgingly told me so when I asked. That meant the last three days had evaporated. I had no recollection of what I said, did, or saw from the time I left my family until the time I awakened in Smithfield Park.

More importantly, I wanted not to care. I wanted to do as instructed by a man that I once gave a nickel to when I was ten: "Boy if you can't 'member nothin' else in life 'member this. Don't never give-ah-fuck 'bout nothin'. Then nothin' can fuck you."

If I were granted one wish, I would catapult myself back to Vietnam and die. That way Fredrika could have continued her life without me. My parents could remember the young man who left instead of the bum who returned. All who knew me could maintain the respect they had for "that Johnson boy," speculating on how prosperous a future I was destined to have had I lived.

"Would've, could've, should've," I thought out loud, "ain't going change shit now."

The ticket clerk glared at me. I averted my gaze toward the square clock over the ticket counter. The lazy hands on the clock read 7:22. My bus was scheduled to leave at 9:15. I looked down at my hand, the one holding the bus ticket. Beaver Falls, One Way, the ticket had printed at the top.

STORY EIGHTEEN

Not a sound short of thunder could have stirred her
-- Fredrika Carletta Booke

The telephone rang. Her eyes opened and stared directly at the noisy device perched atop the battered birch wood dresser. Fredrika refused to answer, refused to move. Her guess was it was Chris making certain she was safe. *Probably calling from work*, she thought, *wanting to be the first to say hello*.

Fredrika slept hard last night. Not a sound short of thunder could have stirred her. Chris had taken her to a small nightclub in East Liberty called The Pyramid for a little dancing and candlelight romancing. They had a few drinks, danced a lot, and met three other couples, not one of whose names she could remember. Chris asked Fredrika to marry him for the countless time. Fredrika surprised herself when she said yes. Now she wondered had she made a mistake.

The telephone kept ringing. Its clamor bounced from wall to ceiling, room to room of the old, small, quiet house on Kilmore Street.

Fredrika made a noise similar to a sigh. It was Saturday. Fredrika diluted the ringing with thoughts of Chris. He was special. Even Gratey's mother had said so. Josephine Johnson told Fredrika that she would snatch Chris up in a second if she were her. "A man who's always there when you need him, treats kids that ain't his like his own. Helps keep house, never forgets birthdays. You even told me he remembers the day you two met, where you were, and what you were wearing. I love my son but he ain't right. That Vietnam thing got him all messed up. If I were you, Freddie, next time Chris asks you to marry him, I'd say yes. That man's one for life and ain't many of them out there. If you don't marry him some right-thinking woman's going to."

Finally the ringing stopped. Fredrika rolled onto her back and stared at the ceiling, following a line of plaster tape to the wall opposite the end of the bed. The house was quiet, serene. Fredrika wondered if death held for her a tranquil dwelling where her soul could settle, permanently freed from earthly suffering. Fredrika could find out. Take the inevitable one-way trip. She certainly had no fear of it. What about her kids, her folks, Chris, the Johnsons, even Gratey? How would they react to her taking her own life? What would they do or say? But Fredrika was tired, worn out from being responsible and caring, burdened with everyday life decisions, especially the basic question of choosing to live. She wanted to vanish as if she never existed and bypass this phase of soul training. Leap into the next stage of development. Maybe that was where she belonged?

Fredrika did not love Chris in the way she still cared for Gratey. That was where the problem germinated. Fredrika desired to be again the way she was when Gratey and she were together, to become giddy and light inside from the sound of his voice. To feel silly when she playfully told one of her awful jokes that Gratey would woefully shake his head at. To tread in kisses that were preludes to mighty pulses of passion that ripped to her center. Never had she felt that way with Chris. Not once had he made her feel out of control. What was the sense in marrying him if she could not give her all? Chris deserved better.

Her first impulse was to close her eyes and return to sleep. Escape for even a brief while. All she could do was think of Gratey and how much Godfrey resembled him. Godfrey had Gratey's eyes, hands, mouth, and hair. That is where -- thankfully -- the resemblance stopped. Fredrika was grateful Godfrey did not have to go through a war like the one Gratey suffered. Although, she realized the streets had their own battle zones.

As Fredrika got up the twin bed squeaked. *It's as tired as me*, she thought about the bed, sliding her swollen feet into her pink foam slippers, and then slipping on her corduroy bathrobe. A smidgen of Chris was in the air a la Brut. *I should call him so he doesn't worry*, she thought.

Fredrika stood, stretched, made the bed with as much conscious effort as winding a watch. Even with the bedroom drapes drawn, she knew the day was gray. Suddenly, the silent house did not seem tranquil. It became a vision of her possible future. Alone in a house with no one, Fredrika looked around the room. With all its furnishings, it was empty. Her stomach became tight like the beginning of menstrual cramps. Above all else she feared being old and alone. But was that enough of a reason to marry Chris?

Fredrika walked down the narrow hallway leading to the top of the living room stairs. Godfrey's bedroom door was open. She bent over and picked up a pair of high-top Nikes collapsed in his doorway. His room was chaos. She looked around and fought the urge to scream. To say it was junky would have been a compliment. *That child of mine*, Fredrika thought, *wait 'til he gets home.*

She would scold her youngest with finger wagging and angry words. Tell him not to leave the house again until his room was clean to her satisfaction and for him to keep it that way. He would clean up his room. Maintain it for a week -- two if his life was uneventful for a while which was seldom with Godfrey. Then gradually, as if a device designed to create disorder in stages were hidden somewhere in his room, the disaster would return.

No matter what he did, especially now, Godfrey was her favorite. He would be out on a date and call home, "Yo moms, this is Godfrey, you all right?" Fredrika would tell him everything was fine. Then he would ask if she wanted the telephone number where he was. She would reassure him a second time everything was fine and order him to get on with his date. There would be a brief moment of silence that suggested to Fredrika that Godfrey didn't believe his mother was telling him the truth, but he did as instructed.

A large cockroach lazily crawled up the wall past the kitchen telephone near the sink. Fredrika recognized him. "R.W." stood for "Roach Warrior." Godfrey nicknamed him that. They tried everything to kill him: Black Flag, Raid, D-con, even Roach-Pruf, nothing worked. For a few days, there would be no sign of him. When you believed him dead, he would dash across the kitchen counter or pop his antennae head out of a small crack around the sink. He always survived. "Give me some of what you got," Fredrika said. "Help me make it through this life."

"Good Lord, I'm losing it," Fredrika said. "I'm talking to a cockroach. Probably a dead head one at that." Fredrika stood hoping to sneak up on R.W. The pest froze, and then quickly vanished behind the kitchen cabinets. Fredrika shook her head and sat down.

Once, Fredrika saw a man preaching on a downtown street corner who looked familiar to her. She was surprised to discover it was Gratey. Fredrika had not seen or heard from Gratey in years and had assumed he had left town again. With the way he was dressed and that ugly beard, she didn't recognize him. But the voice was unmistakable. It made her quiver.

Fredrika ducked into Kaufmann's and watched The Prophet through the glass doors. Seeing Gratey that way made her ache with pity. Fredrika wanted to talk to him, find out where he was staying, what he'd been doing, was there anything she could do? Before Fredrika could discover the courage, a police car came and took him away. All she could do was watch and let it be.

Her father said Fredrika should forget about Gratey, called him a "knuckle-head who ain't good for shit no more." Her father told her he couldn't "understand how she could go on loving a man who disrespected her in the way that he did."

They argued. Fredrika defended her feelings using the attitude her father still held for her mother as Exhibit A. Mr. Booke denied any resemblance and persisted his daughter was wasting her life waiting on "that burned-out moron" any longer. Fredrika learned never to mention Gratey's name around her father. In return, her father ignored the fact Gratey existed.

Fredrika believed deep down her father understood. They were both fools, loving people who could not or would not love them in the way they deserved to be loved. Fredrika was the one who kept letting Gratey back into her life, battle-scarred, abusive, drunk, and smelling of other women. Then he ran away. Now, she wondered. If he returned to her, would she accept him back? Even if he begged her forgiveness for all the wrongs he had done was it worth risking her heart again. All Fredrika wanted for the moment was for Gratey to hold her. Squeeze her close like he did when she was a love-struck girl being romanced by a handsome, witty young man. Her fingers found the locket. For a moment she was sixteen again. Fredrika let the moment pass, unclasped the locket, and left it on the table.

STORY NINETEEN

Love at first sight is an enigma
-- Marcus Douglas Stallworth

It was 11:21 p.m. on a Thursday night. Marcus Stallworth navigated his utility cart down the carpeted hall of the law firm Purcella, Brown, Greenluck, and Clover for the last time. In the stark fluorescent light, Marcus looked military in his sharply creased slate-gray janitorial uniform. The oval nametag embroidered with red thread to his left breast pocket had faded from repeated machine washings. The black thread on a white background reading "MARCUS" was dull and unraveling. White hair, white mustache, taupe skin, and narrow dark brown eyes were the flesh of the man. He moved slower than usual, his slightly stooped back and pigeon toes making him appear burdened by the inevitable finality of that irrevocable day.

The news had arrived three months earlier with no warning. An innocent-looking letter placed in with his paycheck. Marcus thought little of it. He worked swing shift. All of the graveyard and swing shift personnel received management communications in that manner. After he read the letter during his lunch break, he was dumbfounded. Marcus was being let go after thirty-one years with Plateau Janitorial Services. At least that was his interpretation. The letter went on to explain:

"This unfortunate request is in no way indicative of your work with Plateau Janitorial Services. You are highly regarded by management and your peers for your exceptional skills and many years of dedicated service. However, temporary cleaning services are able to undercut our bids. We cannot continue to compete under our current operating conditions. Due to decreasing demands for our services, the company is forced to streamline its work force. I felt it only sensible to ask those employees who have the most years of

144

continuous service to accept early retirement. If you accept, you will walk away with extended benefits and a pension corresponding to your years of service per your employment agreement. Let me be candid here. If you should decline, I cannot guarantee how much longer we can stay in business without your cooperation. As much as I hate to pressure you, those are the facts. In any case, whatever you should decide, I wish you the best of luck.

"Robert Simms, President"

Marcus knew the drill. Simms expected little resistance to his request. In part, because what he said about temporary janitorial services were true. Secondly, the court costs alone to fight him would make it too expensive a risk for any old-timer. Even if Marcus won, it would be little more than a moral victory. With no labor union to protect them, Simms would manufacture other reasons to fire any undesirable employee.

Marcus felt he should have seen it coming. Since Robert Simms had taken over Plateau from his deceased father, Marcus believed he had two things in mind: eradicating the labor union and increasing company profits through cheaper labor. Fifty-eight percent of the Plateau janitorial staff were under twenty-five. Most of them were people who would move in and out of janitorial work. Another twenty-two percent had been with Plateau between five to twelve years. The majority of them were middle-aged. Old-timers were in short supply. They were also the highest paid. After Simms convinced the youthful majority of the obsolescence, and possible corruption, of their labor union, he patiently implemented his plan.

For the first couple of years, Simms took extraordinary care of his employees. Giving few pause to believe they had made a mistake ousting the labor union. Even Marcus was beginning to have doubts regarding Robert Simms' motives. Then suddenly, as if by overnight, the Robert Simms of old emerged again. Benefits were cut in half. Merit raises were frozen. Sick leave hours took twice as long to earn. A flat vacation rate of two weeks per year was instituted for full-time hourly employees regardless of seniority. A number of the mid-range janitors left. A few of the seniors opted for early retirement. The rest decided to ride it out due to a lack of viable alternatives. With one child in graduate school and two in undergraduate, ten years left on a house mortgage, two car notes and car insurance, Marcus could not afford the pay cut. He fell into the last category.

Marcus parked his utility cart just outside the large corner office of Daniel J. Clover, Senior Partner. He plucked the feather duster sprouting from his hip pocket before entering. Marcus began with the desk. Taking meticulous care to place each item back where it originally rested. He had seen that office change hands five times over the last three decades. One business would move out, another would move in before the dust settled. Marcus never dreamed that his day would come so soon, and when it did, certainly not in the form of a thinly veiled extortion.

A photograph of a woman who Marcus assumed was Mrs. Clover brought to mind his wife. *Sweet bubbling brown sugar*, that was his opening thought when Marcus first laid eyes upon Lorraine at the veterans Administration. Marcus had been honorably discharged from the Navy and was there to investigate his veteran's benefits. Lorraine worked as an administrative assistant in a pool of such employees. There was not much chocolate in the milk so she was easy to spot. That was why Marcus noticed her. It was not why he continued to stare.

Her walk, her dress, her style, and her figure mesmerized Marcus. As Lorraine passed near the director's office where Marcus awaited his return, he had a good look at her face. Lorraine put him in mind of a young Diahann Carroll. She had the same mocha complexion, tight firm mouth, silky-looking skin, alluring eyes, petite nose, and rounded chin and cheeks. Under the office lights, her thick jet-black hair shone, and was as soft as mink, Marcus would later discover.

With an engaging smile, Lorraine had said hello in passing. Her naturally sensual voice exhilarated Marcus in a way that he had never before experienced. It made his heart palpitate and his blood pressure rise. When his palms began to sweat, he sensed he had entered new territory. Since love had never fallen into his lap, Marcus was uncertain Lorraine was the one. Time would cure him of his doubt.

Love at first sight is an enigma. Lust is a constant tremor in men. To distinguish the higher calling of one over the yelping yearnings of the other is rather difficult -- at times impossible. It is only after the craving has yielded, the hyperactive gnawing voice subsided, that the heart's message can come through.

With Lorraine, Marcus would experience both. Lorraine would have none of his fire without a firm pillow to rest her head when their flames quelled. Marcus tried. More than once and with every trick he could muster. Lorraine saw through them all. Nothing worked short of honest expressions of love. Each of her sensuous kisses told him so. As did her vibrant touch, sincere smile, and wet whispers that made his stomach fill with butterflies and his breath to quicken. How could Lorraine tell his dream love of his misfortune, of their misfortune? It would be easier to toss himself from the dizzying height of the U.S. Steel Building than give Lorraine cause to shed one tear.

Their lives were not supposed to proceed as they had. By the time Marcus and Lorraine were married, Marcus was in his second year at Robert Morris College. Business Management was his major. It was during his sophomore year they had their first child, Tanya. Both he and Lorraine agreed, she would quit her job and become a full-time mom and housekeeper. Marcus took on a part-time position with Plateau to supplement his VA benefits and partially replace Lorraine's absent income. It also allowed Marcus to continue his education on a part-time basis. Two years later, Luther was born. By then Marcus had already hired on full-time with Plateau. Money had taken precedence. Marcus put his education on hold, or so he thought. Martin was born three years after Luther. They had already moved into a house and bought a car. Most things were more expensive than they had imagined, the cost of living, literally, kept Marcus at Plateau. Marcus was locked into what is known as the golden cage. He didn't mind. He was only after the degree for the money anyway. It turned out janitorial work paid better than he realized.

Now the carpet was being ripped out from under him. He had not yet told Lorraine about his forced retirement. Since their youngest entered high school, Lorraine had returned to work as a part-time administrative assistant with the NAACP. They mostly put away her wages for a rainy day. There was no telling how many rainy days lie ahead for the Stallworths.

Marcus finished dusting. He returned the feather duster to his hip pocket, and then went to the utility cart to dump the wastebasket and grab the spray cleaner and a couple of cleaning rags. Once again, he began with the desk. Spritzing anything made of glass or plastic then polishing it until it shined.

It came without fanfare five weeks ago. A large brown envelope marked "URGENT! OFFICIAL DOCUMENTS ENCLOSED. DO NOT DISCARD." Marcus had tried such contests before without winning as much as a consolation prize. Still he opened it, fully expecting another disappointment. That was before he saw what was inside.

The contents were highly suggestive the sweepstakes' winners had been narrowed down to two people in the entire state of Pennsylvania, Marcus and a person by the name of Clarice Fulmaker. There was even a garish winner's certificate with "Marcus Stallworth" printed on it included with the materials. One letter made it clear, if he were delinquent sending in his confirmation entry, then Clarice Fulmaker would be next in line to win the grand prize he so thoughtlessly forfeited.

Marcus did what needed to be done to enter the sweepstakes, following the instructions to the letter. Heeding the advice in one of the letters, he subscribed to a couple of magazines he did not either want or need as a courtesy in spite of mild objections from Lorraine. He agreed with the statement that implied it would look better, after being presented with a check the size of himself, if he could answer, yes, when asked if he had taken advantage of some of their magazine subscription offers. *A small price to pay to become an instant multimillionaire*, Marcus thought.

At the beginning, Marcus held high hopes of winning. As his concluding days of employment approached, those hopes had agitated into a distorted expectation. This was the weekend the money was to be awarded. Marcus had come to believe he truly was the one. So much so, he had invited close friends and neighbors by for a Sunday barbecue as witnesses to the event. He did not inform them of his motive. Not even Lorraine knew. How else could they appear surprised when the Sweepstakes Patrol dropped in to present him with a five-million-dollar check?

Then there was the question of what to do with all of that money. Pay off his bills. Secure his children's education. Take a cruise. Buy Lorraine some of those extravagances she has always talked about having like a mink coat and a diamond necklace. Buy himself a small fishing boat. Donate to a few of their favorite charities, and one act of mercy.

Marcus and Lorraine had known the Johnsons for six years before Gratey was born. They were good neighbors. Close neighbors. Marcus was the first one there when he heard Josephine Johnson scream. Lorraine remained at home. The door was unlocked. He burst in. What he saw will forever remain darkly ingrained in his memory.

It was chaos. Carl Johnson was on his knees near the crib, holding the limp body of Camille, imploring her to make a sound. Josephine had collapsed onto the floor wailing and crying, wearing nothing, afraid to go near her baby. Gratey was in teary-eyed shock, propped up against the Johnson's bedroom door. There was a wood block with a metal rod sticking out of it, crimson blood smeared on both. It was Camille's blood. Marcus had no difficulty ascertaining what had happened.

The first thing Marcus did was rush over and check Camille for vitals. She was gone. Blood was still dripping from the puncture wound in her head. Marcus rushed to close the front door. Then he hurried into the Johnsons' bedroom for a blanket to cover Josephine. Marcus tried convincing Gratey to wait at his place to get him away from that gruesome scene. Gratey refused. Gratey blubbered about it all being his fault, saying how he should be the one dead, not Camille. Marcus managed to calm Gratey enough to persuade him to go to his room. Marcus then telephoned the police. Immediately afterwards, Marcus telephoned Lorraine emphasizing for her not to come over for reasons he would explain later.

The police were quick to rule Camille's death an accident. No one suspected otherwise. Josephine managed to pull herself together long enough to convince Carl to hand over his daughter's corpse to the medical examiner. No sooner did Carl let go of Camille than he broke down and cried. He and Josephine wallowed in their despair, in each other's arms. No one noticed when Gratey disappeared.

Marcus was concerned. He went looking for Gratey. He found him on the roof of the Johnsons' three-story home. Gratey was standing near the edge facing the backyard, sobbing. He talked about jumping. The police had already left. Marcus inched his way toward Gratey. Marcus spent the better part of an hour trying to convince Gratey to live. When Marcus was within arm's reach, he grabbed Gratey, holding on to him until they reached ground zero.

It was not easy for the Johnsons for some time afterwards, especially for Gratey. Marcus understood his pain. That was why he repeatedly tried talking to Gratey, The Prophet, about his antics. Gratey always remembered Marcus. Gratey was invariably polite to him. He listened. Gratey would not explain to Marcus why he carried on in such a manner. He only said, "It's the Lord's will." Marcus tried to convince Gratey there were other ways, better ways. Nothing seemed to work. Marcus always left Gratey hoping he would change his mind. Change his ways. With his newfound wealth, Marcus was willing to pay for Gratey to get professional help. If Gratey would not accept his help, Marcus hoped Gratey would at least allow him to buy him a respectable wardrobe.

The sound of a vacuum cleaner made its way down the hall. Marcus was done with the corner office. He quietly exited closing the door behind him. That was the cue that the room had been cleaned. It was clear to vacuum. Brad was running the vacuum. He was one of the MTV generation. He smiled at Marcus. *A friendly smile from a good kid*, Marcus thought, *a bright kid just out of high school*. Taking a break from the books as Brad put it. He was listening to a rap song, bobbing his dreadlocks to the electronic beat. Marcus could hear it through his headphones. In a year, Marcus expected Plateau to be a full-blown temp agency. *If you can't beat 'em, join 'em*, he thought. *No benefits, no medical*, his thoughts continued, *paying barely above minimum wage, if that*. Marcus expected Brad would have moved on well before the official metamorphosis occurred. In his heart, he wished Brad well. He wished him a loving and prosperous future.

Marcus put his utility cart away for the final time saddened as if saying goodbye to a dear old friend. He would return his uniforms to Plateau within the two-week stipulation period. Had it not been for his impending wealth, Marcus would have been anxious about his future and that of his family. Winning the sweepstakes was assured in his mind. It was just as certain as pits in a peach. Although he apprehended wealth had problems of its own, Marcus was certain it was not anything he could not handle. He was confident adjusting to being rich would be a cinch. It had to be a lot easier than working for a living.

STORY TWENTY

Whom do we blame
-- The Prophet

"Before anything existed, there was Christ, with God. He has always been alive and is Himself God. He created everything there is -- nothing exists that he didn't make. Eternal life is in Him, and this life gives light to all mankind. His life is the light that shines through the darkness -- and the darkness can never extinguish it."

When "The Way" fell open to the Book of John, my eyes immediately magnetized to those words, I read on. "God sent John the Baptist as a witness to the fact that Jesus Christ is the true light. John himself was not the Light: he was only a witness to identify it."

Each passage I consumed as a sinful fated man in dreadful search for a liberating last penance. Nothing escaped my comprehension. I felt invigorated, connected to something alive and positive. Wait a minute, that all happened some time ago in the Celestial Book Store after I first saw the light.

When I left Fredrika and the kids, I left Pittsburgh. Bummed around the country, losing myself in one place after another long enough to make a few dollars to move on.

It was interesting. I learned a little about people. More importantly, I found out I wasn't the only 'Nam vet hurting. Everywhere I went, there were at least a handful of us bitching about the war, government, civilians, wives, girlfriends, kids, money, jobs, the whole tragic deal. Didn't seem right the way we were being treated. But like most of us, I didn't do shit about it.

After years of self-exile, I found myself back in Pittsburgh. My dad and I hadn't been getting along when I left. My father didn't like the way I treated Fredrika, neither did he care for the fact I was always drunk and high and looked like a bum, a bum who couldn't hold down any kind of job for more than a month.

Mom had come to accept me as damaged goods and was doing her best to live with that. Dad wasn't having any of it. He tried a more patient, passive approach to helping me change my life when I returned from my hiatus. His advice and positive guidance were framed in diplomatic tones. Every effort my father made to help me I pretty much spit back in his face. It was the anger talking. I didn't realize it then. A constant vomiting of all the rancid meals life had served me since my tour of duty in 'Nam, most of which I spewed on the people who cared most about me.

My father lost his patience. We picked up where we left off. We nearly came to blows. He called me a bum, a wine head, and a whore-chasing sorry-ass loser. Said all I wanted to do was cry about Vietnam. My dad told me point blank, "If you ever set foot inside my house again you'd better send your soul to Jesus because your ass will belong to me."

"Fuck you dad!" That's what I screamed at my father with my mother looking on. Turned my back and walked away.

I stayed clear of my parents for about a year. Pretty much lived on the street during that time. Then I met the Reverend Theodore Joshua Palmer. He saw me flat on my back, half-conscious in some doorway after an all-night binge. The reverend asked if there was anything he could do to help. I told him, "Yeah, get me a drink." He said that was out of the question, but he would give me shelter. I didn't know then my mother had talked to Reverend Palmer about me. Mom had asked for his help and he had promised to do what he could.

I looked sideways at this preacher, a small man who stood comfortably erect, with round, roaming eyes that seemed capable of witnessing everything. He was bald on top with a horseshoe of silver-black hair that reached from ear to ear. He smiled. It was a nice smile, seemed innocent enough. "What kind of freak is this?" I mumbled to myself half-dazed eyeing the man without his collar. Reverend Palmer reached out his hand. I took it.

Reverend Palmer took me into his home, gave me a room, clothing and hot meals. All he asked in return was that I help out at one of the five Holy Mission shelters that he sponsored, and clean his

Ebenezer Baptist Church once a week. That man showed me what it was like to all-out care about someone and expect next to nothing in return. The Reverend didn't just preach Christianity; he lived it.

To show the unique way that the Lord works, one: Ebenezer Baptist is only half a block up the street from where my parents live. Two: Reverend Palmer married my parents. Three: Reverend Palmer gave the eulogy at Camille's funeral.

To show how messed up I was, I didn't remember the latter two things until I was reunited with my parents. They refreshed my memory on the good reverend.

With Reverend Palmer's help, I tried piecing some kind of life together out of all the shrapnel I had created. I stopped using drugs, cut back on my drinking, and reintroduced myself to good hygiene. I saved a little money from working odd jobs that I found around the city. Got some decent clothes and a pair of dress shoes and, most importantly, I found the courage to go and see my parents.

For the first time in ages, I told my mother and father how much I loved them. They were finally able to confess that they blamed me for Camille's death. I cried, apologized, and begged for their forgiveness. They said they already had. When our mutual grieving was exhausted, the void was closed. I still hurt about what happened to Camille. I always will. Only now I can live with the pain not slowly die from it. You could say I was on my way to finding peace.

Fortunately for me, Fredrika had stayed in touch with my parents because I couldn't find her or her father when I got back. My parents refused to tell me where Fredrika had moved. Mom said whether Freddie wanted to see me was a decision she had to make. What could I say? My mother was right.

When I heard this excited girlish voice on the phone, I knew it was Fredrika. I was so overwhelmed to hear from her, I was almost speechless. Fredrika invited me over to see her and the kids. I accepted her invitation with a tinge of reluctance. It had been a long time, and to be honest I didn't know what to expect.

Clean and sober and nervous, wearing my only suit, I showed up with a dozen love-in-a-mist and toys for the kids. Fredrika looked fantastic. Her face was smooth, radiant, and full, just like when we were in high school. I handed her the flowers and gifts and told Fredrika how great she looked. Fredrika smiled that bashful smile and ushered me inside.

We wound up in the dining room because Fredrika wanted me to herself for a bit. "Before the kids get a-hold of you," as she put it.

Fredrika told me how she had gone to secretarial school and earned a certificate of some kind. At that time, she was working as a secretary for U.S. Steel. I told Fredrika of how proud I was of her, and how glad I was that she was doing okay. Fredrika gave me one of her kindly stares. Everything seemed frozen just then. We were in a fixed state, seeing each other as we were, or believed we should've been. I imagined that was the way Fredrika always saw me. It made me sad.

After an hour or so of listening to Fredrika catch me up on her life (and five minutes of me telling her about mine), the mother of my children led me into the living room, introduced me, and left me alone with our kids.

God that was tough. I gave them rather awkward greetings that they returned in kind. I sat in this puffy reading chair across from the couch, stiff-backed, staring at those beautiful faces. Each of them had grown so much. They were strangers to me, remotely attached by some memory collage. I couldn't think of anything to say, and apparently they couldn't either. I racked the mush I had left for brains, searching for any reason why I belonged there. "What could I possibly offer them that was worth anything?" I kept asking myself. The answer, no matter how I sugared it, came out not a damn thing.

A few hours later I was still sitting there as silent as a monk, feeling no closer to my children than I had when I rang the doorbell. Looking back, it was clear those moments were a sign from above. Quietly I left, telling the kids how and where to get in touch with me anytime they needed me. Nat was the only one who took me up on it. Now I hear he's dealing dope.

I tried stopping by to check on things every now and then. Fredrika was dating an attorney. From what Fredrika told me, he seemed like a nice person, although I never met him. The kids called him dad. Me they called Gratey. That hurt. It would've been less painful to be skinned alive.

Fredrika never tried to stop me from visiting. She never mentioned for me to stay away. She didn't have to. We both came to realize what was best for everyone involved. I told Nat not to come around anymore in terms my son could only accept as nonnegotiable. I stopped seeing the love of my life and our children. It was time to let go. My big dream bit the dust.

The night after I told Nat not to come around was a Friday. I went to clean the church as always. Only this time I had an assistant, half a pint of gin.

I did the floors, pulpit, choir stand, organ and was dusting the pews when I decided to take a breather. All night I had taken healthy sips of my assistant. Polished two-thirds of the bottle off and was looking to knock out the last of it. Guaranteed, I wasn't feeling any pain.

The church was locked up tight I had made sure of that. I sat down in one of the back pews and took a couple of healthy swigs. I was exhausted. You know the kind of fatigue that burrows into the very core of your being. A wasted feeling, absent of hope and care. I just plain felt like giving up.

Stretched out on the pew, figured I'd rest for a minute and I'd be okay. I must've passed out.

Out of the distance, I heard this stern heavy voice. When I opened my eyes, the first thing I saw was the painting on the ceiling of the church, a black African Christ rising toward heaven with a rainbow of angels encircling him. My first presumption was it was the voice of Christ speaking to me:

"Every single day another bushel of souls deprive themselves of the glorious bounty of heaven."

I shook my head, raised the gin bottle to my lips. The cap was screwed down tight so nothing came out. *A sign The Lord is talking to you. He don't want nothing standing in the way of you and his words.* That's what I'd thought. I shoved the gin bottle back into my pocket and listened.

"Whom do you blame, certainly not ourselves. Satan you say. Perhaps, but we know Lucifer to be the enemy don't we? So who does the burden of responsibility lie upon for our souls to reach the Promised Land?"

As I listened, there was something familiar about the voice. I propped myself up on my elbows enough to barely see the pulpit over the backs of the pews. Reverend Palmer was up there wearing his favorite gray cardigan sweater practicing his Sunday sermon. His voice had a sense of foreboding that made me feel as if he were directly addressing me. I believed I had to listen. I eased myself back down and did just that.

Reverend Palmer went on to tell the story of how Judas betrayed Christ and how Christ understood and forgave him. I didn't show myself. I didn't want the reverend to know I had been sleeping and drinking in church. He wouldn't have liked that at all.

The whole sermon lasted maybe twenty minutes. I had read the story of Judas a few times. It never really struck home until Reverend Palmer finished.

"If Christ can forgive those who committed the greatest sin against him, can we not be a fraction as forgiving of our sisters and brothers and ourselves. Christen thy life as you would a baby. Then God will forever be your guardian and his words your salvation. Go from here and start anew."

That's when I truly first saw the Light.

Maybe I needed to suffer the way I did to find the Lord and hold onto him. So many people lose faith for lesser reasons. Only call upon him when things go wrong or it's convenient. "The righteous path is not often paved and narrow. The way to God is not often lighted and sure. But he is always there and ever true; for those who are true to him." Reverend Palmer said those very words at church this past Sunday. And I do believe.

Since I've found "The Way," I haven't strayed. It's my purpose in life. God took me along that disastrous road to prove to me man is wrong. His way cannot work. Only He is the Light and the Truth there is no other. Until man returns to Him, he will forever suffer the agony of his stubbornness.

So I preach. Dressed like a maniac and behaving like one. I holler, point, and in short put on a show. My only wish is that some will listen. Not necessarily to me (I wouldn't listen to a man dressed the way I am and behaving as I do). But if while they're driving home, or riding a bus, or sitting in a bar, having dinner, watching TV, snorting a line, hanging out on the streets, pushing, pimping, whoring, fighting, scuffling to survive, something I've said resonates with them, maybe that will launch the beginning of their repentance. Before the coffin closes and it's too late.

I stepped out from Kaufmann's clock to the curb roughly brushing aside anyone in my way.

"Step lively you sinners," I bellowed, "or the fiery brimstone of hell will scorch your feet! The Lord has a vigilant eye on you!"

"Get away from me man." A stocky young man with menace in his eyes said to me as he stood next to me on the corner. His face was puckered as if he'd taken a bite out of something that had a disgusting flavor.

"Stand clear of me boy," I warned glaring down at him. "God bids me to speak and I will do so. All who defy me defy the Lord. And that will not be tolerated."

With a quick two-step, the boy hurried across the street looking wide-eyed over his shoulder at me.

Dark clouds had gathered. The sweet scent of summer rain was in the swirling air. Thunder rumbled, getting louder with each powerful roar. People rushed around me with their minds set on distinct purposes and distant destinations; fewer noticing me, fewer hearing my words.

THE END

CPSIA information can be obtained at www.ICGtesting.com
Printed in the USA
BVOW04s0255100615

403513BV00004B/125/P